CANYON OF TEARS

For forty years, Mexican comancheros and Comanche Indians have brought terror to west Texas frontier settlements. Their latest victim, beautiful Rose Cahill, is snatched by the evil bandido Joaquin Terrazos. Only a few days before, Rose had lost her heart to the Texas Ranger Chas Dawson, but will he still want her after the comancheros have done with her? The US Army are refusing to help, so Captain Dawson enlists fourteen-year-old Pete Bowen and they go out alone to search for the girl.

Books by John Dyson
in the Linford Western Library:

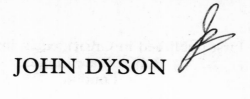

JOHN DYSON

CANYON
OF
TEARS

Complete and Unabridged

LINFORD
Leicester

First published in Great Britain in 2000 by
Robert Hale Limited
London

First Linford Edition
published 2001
by arrangement with
Robert Hale Limited
London

British Library CIP Data

Dyson, John, *1943 –*
Canyon of tears.—Large print ed.—
Linford western library
1. Western stories
2. Large type books
I. Title
823.9'14 [F]

ISBN 0–7089–9717–1

Published by
F. A. Thorpe (Publishing)
Anstey, Leicestershire

Set by Words & Graphics Ltd.
Anstey, Leicestershire
Printed and bound in Great Britain by
T. J. International Ltd., Padstow, Cornwall

This book is printed on acid-free paper

1

He rode out of a red haze of dust, driving a dozen mustangs before him, and at first Rose Cahill thought it was her husband, Jake, who had set off for Fort Worth that day. But, no, Jake did not wear a tall sombrero. The dark silhouette was that of a Mexican, the lowering sun at his back glinting on the silver inlay of his bridle and the long-barrelled revolver that hung on his hip.

'*Buenas tardes.*' The sun glinted on gold teeth, too, as the Mexican shouted at her. 'Open your corral.'

Surprised, Rose ran from the kitchen door of their adobe homestead to do so, impressed by the way the rider controlled the surge of half-broken mustangs by loud snaking cracks of his six-foot rawhide bullwhip, driving them skittering through the gate posts. 'Are

1

these for us?' Ingenuous, she replaced the pole and looked up at him as the dust cleared. 'Jake never said.'

'You wan? You haff.' The rider's lip curled back over his glinting teeth and his eyes smouldered with lechery as he looked down at the young woman, pert and pretty beneath a mass of bouncing dark curls. His eyes lingered on her embonpoint in the tight-waisted calico dress. 'Whass you trade?'

'Trade? I don't know. We certainly have no cash.' Rose looked the restless mustangs over. They were fine-fettled stock. 'What do you want?'

'Wha' do hy wan'?' The Mexican's face was disfigured by a white scar across one cheek, vivid even in the shade of the wide sombrero. He jumped down lightly, let his mustang head towards the wooden water trough, and walked past her into the cabin unin-vited. 'Wha' you got?'

'Hey, you can't just — ' Rose eyed their rifle propped against the cabin wall, but the Mexican was between them. 'What are you doing?'

The rider was slapping his leather-clad thigh with the coiled bullwhip and, with his other gloved hand was picking up various household implements, examining them with interest. He appeared particularly impressed by her large copper kettle and their pewter plates and mugs, milk-jug, sugar basin and salt cellar on the table. '*Bueno*,' he said, indicating them with a sweep of his hand. 'You trade?'

'I — I don't know. I'll have to ask my husband. He — he — ll be back soon.'

'No, he back *mañana*. I see him go. He take trail to fort.'

'But, these things, we need them.'

'Pah! You soon buy plenty more. Thees horse, they valuable.' He pushed past her and went into their bedroom. On the dressing-table with its mirror was a scattering of bracelets, necklaces, ear bobs, an imitation silver reticule. Not expensive, just cheap feminine geegaws. The Mexican swept them up in his hand and brandished them at her.

He pointed his whip at a copper-framed mirror. 'Thiss. Thass. An' stuff in there.' He indicated the living-room. 'We trade. *Si*?'

'No!' she cried, sharply. 'I don't know. Can't you come back tomorrow?'

'*Caballos mio.*' He tapped his chest. 'No *barato*. No come back. I got go.' His face was as dark and hard-cut as the mahogany of their bedroom furniture. And the pupils of his eyes, too, were two dark pinpoints, smouldering with a mocking enquiry. 'Whass you say?' He tossed the geegaws back on the dressing-table, pulled off a glove and reached out a hand to stroke her cheek. Rose tried to step back, the sour smell of his sweat in her nostrils, but she was up against the wall and could not do so. 'You — *tu estas hermosa. Bonita! Muy buena!*' He glanced, significantly, at the neatly made bed, and his hard, horny hand gripped her chin and held it high. 'You hussband lucky man.'

'Don't touch me,' she hissed. 'If he

knew he would kill you.'

'He could *try* keel me!' The man tossed his head arrogantly, releasing her. 'Eef he find me.'

Rose slipped away back into the other room, her heart fluttering, her legs and arms weak and unsteady. All she wanted was to get rid of him. The Mexican laughed, harshly, and helped himself to a ladle of water from the wooden bucket. 'You got nice place, eh?' He picked up two needlework antimacassars from their chairs, took a pokerwork Biblical quote from the wall, 'Rest Your Burden Upon the Lord'. He grunted and turned to her. 'Thiss, too. Thassall. Horses yours. Good trade, yes?'

'Very well. Yes.' Maybe it was good trade. The horses were worth at least $120 the lot, and their utensils and ornaments a fraction of that. They could easily be replaced. But she just wanted to placate him, be rid of him. She reached for an empty sack, handed it to him. 'Take them and go.'

5

'*Vamos? Si*!' The Mexican threw the chosen items into the sack. The harsh rowels of his spurs clattering, he stomped back into the bedroom and tore aside the curtain of the alcove that served as her wardrobe. There were her dresses, one summer cotton, one gingham, and a dark velvet for best, shawls and blouses. 'Ver' pretty,' he said, fondling them. 'You wan' sell?'

'No.' She plucked the curtain from his hand and swished it back. 'You're not having them.'

'Oh-hay!' he smiled. 'You no fuss. I no have them.' He tossed the trinkets and beads into the bag. 'Oh-hay? You no say I rob you? You no send soldiers after me? Thass fair trade? *Si*?'

'*Si*, yes,' she hurriedly agreed. 'I am happy. Fair trade.'

'You happy? Good.' He strode outside, tied the sack to the saddle horn, glanced furtively around. There was only the empty plain, the distant mountains in their purple dusk. He swung into the saddle and doffed his

6

hand at his hat. '*Adios, señora.* Maybe we meet again.'

'*Adios.*' She watched him ride away at a steady lope, disappear into the red dust haze of the setting sun from which he had come. She released her breath with a sigh of relief and returned to the kitchen, sinking to a chair, resting her head on her hand. 'Oh, God!' She felt like she had narrowly escaped a fate worse than death. 'The insolence of the man. Touching me! Eugh!'

She started to her feet again. She wanted to get her chores done before darkness fell. The door bolted, the windows shuttered, the rifle primed. It would be a long night.

'Why does Jake have to leave me alone?'

★   ★   ★

Rose was a newcomer out on the frontier, for frontier it was in the Year of Our Lord 1858. Their nearest neighbours lived in the little village of Dallas and the stockaded US Army post of Fort Worth was their main bastion of defence. To the west beyond the rivers and row of hills, lay a vast area of plains and escarpments largely unsettled, or even explored by white Texans, the domain of Comanches, a name for the past forty years synonymous with terror.

The cabin was oddly bare without their few possessions, but Rose figured she could replace them through the mail-order catalogue. She, herself, had been a mail-order bride. Jake had written, or had someone write for him, the previous summer in answer to the advertisement she had placed in the catalogue: 'Girl, seventeen, slim, brunette, white, Protestant, considered pretty, can cook, sew, do sums, read, write, seeks young rancher, or farmer, for marriage.'

It had been, in a way, a desperate bid to escape from Liberty, the Texas town she had been born to, escape the nagging rule of her father, a clerk in the tanning works, the claustrophobia of sharing a small home with him and her three unmarried sisters. From the age of fourteen she had sat on a high stool alongside him, totting up figures, the scent of the dark, dank warehouse forever in her nostrils. She had longed, like a bird in a cage, to escape into the wilds.

'I got a hundred acres of fine fertile land on the upper reaches of the Trinity River,' Jake wrote to her, 'and I'm looking for a gal like you to make my respected wife.'

That wasn't so far out there would be any danger. And Rose had set forth in high hopes. It had been a surprise to find Jake wasn't as young as he had sounded, indeed, was already running to fat, and had a wide bald dome over tiny features, but he was frank and honest, and married her in a very matter-of-fact manner in Dallas court-house. They left by buggy for the 'dobe on Pecan Creek and, to be sure, it was not the large ranch-house she had imagined, but it was home. And she had cheerfully set about giving it the feminine touch.

Of course, she had not been brought up to feed hogs, or cure bacon, or milk cows, up before dawn, as Jake ploughed and sowed, but she set to with a will. There was weaving and washing and a hundred and one other jobs to do on a farm, and she was usually exhausted by nightfall. When the first happy honeymoon weeks had passed, and she had settled into a routine, Jake's attitude had changed. He had been exasperated by her squeamishness about wringing a chicken's neck, or her inexperience at plucking, gutting and cooking. 'Cain't you do anything right?' he had moaned at her. Sometimes he was as bullying and as sarcastic as her father. Sometimes she thought she had swapped one prison for another.

However, she was pretty sure, as a new day dawned, he would be pleased with her trade with the Mexican. They could sell the horses and spend twenty dollars on new pots and a mirror. We're gonna make a nice profit, she said to herself.

★ ★ ★

'What in tarnation's been goin' on here?' Jake roared, as he climbed from the buggy. 'What are them hosses doin' in the corral?' He brushed aside her explanation. 'Are you gone stark ravin' mad, gal? Anybody can see from the brand them hosses is stolen.'

Jake was so mad Rose was afraid he might take off his belt and larupp her, as he already had on occasion. But he happened to have another man riding along with him, by the badge on his shirt a Texas Ranger, a grave-faced, clean-shaven young man in buckskin jacket, bandanna and chaps. His grey eyes were stone steady as he studied Rose, her smooth cheeks colouring up with shame. 'I didn't know,' she protested. 'He said they were his. *Mio caballos*. My horses. Those were his words.'

Maybe if the lawman hadn't been there Jake might not have bothered about them being stolen, might have set about changing the brands, getting rid of the horses. Rose was glad of the stranger's presence because, at least, it simmered down Jake's anger as they ushered her into the cabin.

'Didn't you ask to see a bill of sale?' her husband wailed with exasperation. 'Ain't you got any sense?'

'Did he give you his name?' the Ranger asked. 'What did this man look like?'

When Rose described the white gash on his cheek, he growled, 'Joaquin Terrazos! What's he doing as far east as this?'

'You give him Ma's mirror?' Jake howled. 'That was a wedding gift.'

'Did he threaten you? Did he force you?' the Ranger asked.

'Did he do anything to you, Rose?' Jake demanded.

'No,' she faltered. 'He just frightened me a bit. Nothing, really. Just the way he acted.'

'Well he might,' the stranger muttered. 'Terrazos would have little compunction about cutting any man's throat. Or woman's, come to that.'

'I thought I was making a good bargain. Those few household things, they aren't worth much. What good are they to him?'

'To him they're nothing. But to a Comanche those baubles are worth a lot. He'll probably trade them for a hundred horses.'

'Comanche?' Rose was startled. 'But they're not around here.'

'They're not far away,' the Ranger said. 'You've only to cross the Rio Brazos and the Colorado range of hills and the plains are crawling with them. Our friend Joaquin is what they call a *Comanchero*.'

'*Comanchero?*'

'Yeah,' Jake jeered. 'Don't you know nuthin'? They're the ones behind the

13

Comanches' thievin'. They're the ones who trade with 'em, supply 'em with rifles in exchange for stolen horses. Them filthy Mex bandits are the ones behind all the trouble.'

'They've been doing it for years,' the lawman said, more quietly. 'Since the turn of the century, since the Spanish made a treaty with the Comanche.'

'Well, of course I've heard of them.' Rose's speckled amber eyes filled with apprehension. 'But I never expected to meet one on my doorstep.'

'Hot damn. You're lucky to be alive,' Jake snapped. 'You better make yourself useful, go git them sacks of flour off the buggy. This here's Charles Dawson, captain of Texas Rangers. He'll be staying for dinner.'

Dawson touched his wide-brimmed hat. 'If that's amenable to you, ma'am?'

*   *   *

In spite of his hard profession there was something of tenderness in Captain

14

Dawson's pale grey eyes as they met hers across the dinner-table. A concern in them, especially when her husband spoke to her sharply. For seconds he ceased spooning up the turgid beef stew, his knuckles gripping the wooden spoon, as offended as she was by the sarcastic words. But a husband was entitled to speak to his wife as he chose, chastise her if he wished. So he made no remark.

'Seein' as Rose has seen fit to give all our pewter mugs away I guess we'll have to sup coffee outa the pot,' Jake sneered.

'There is a wooden one left,' she said. 'We could pass that round.'

'Pass it round? What kinda hospitality's that?' Jake stuck out his legs, bloated, as Rose cleared the wooden bowls. 'It's a wonder she didn't give the chairs and table away while she was at it.'

'I figure Terrazos has a good start on us now,' the Ranger said. 'Maybe first I'd better go check that those horses were stolen. It's the Diamond O brand. They got a spread along the Little Brazos about thirty miles away.'

'They're stole, all right. Any fool should know that.'

'Let me help you with the dishes Miz Cahill,' Ranger Dawson murmured politely, going to stand beside her at the bowl in the alcove. 'You've had a trying experience.'

'And it don't look like I'll hear the last of it for a long while,' she murmured in reply, and smiled at him, passing a drying cloth.

He did not reply but busied himself. Rose could not help glancing at him curiously. He was a broad-chested young man, with a strong jaw, and a mass of wavy brown hair that fell unruly across his brow and stretched back to the nape of his bandanna. He wore a blue denim cross-over shirt, faded by the sun, and a wide red bandanna loosely knotted. He wore the new riveted Levi jeans, chaps, high-heel boots and spurs of a horseman.

He had rolled up his sleeves and at one point as he reached, his bare arm touched hers. To Rose it was like the tingle of an electric current. She had never experienced the like with a man before. For a moment she let the touch linger, pressing against him, and blushed as she turned to him, and met his eyes. It was as if he could read her thoughts, as if he knew that she was wishing he was the kind of man who had sent for her mail order.

Jake was bellowing, 'How long you gonna be with that coffee?' And Rose made a smiling grimace. 'Don't worry about my husband,' she murmured. 'He don't mean nuthin' by it.'

'It's not him I'm worried about,' Dawson said. 'It's you. With this man Terrazos about I think you should go into the fort.'

'You hear what the captain says, Jake? He thinks we should go into the fort for safety.'

'How can we do that? Who's gonna look after the stock? Don't come up

17

with any more stupid ideas.'

'It's not that stupid, Jake. If you won't go, I think your wife should be protected until we've run Terrazos out of the vicinity.'

'She's safe enough with me. I ain't havin' her sittin' on her butt in Fort Worth when there's work to be done.'

After they had supped coffee out of wooden bowls, Captain Dawson said he would ride overnight to the Diamond O ranch and check out Terrazos's story. Then he would look for his trail. 'So long,' Jake called, not bothering to get up from in front of the fire.

Rose went outside to the water-pump and watched the Ranger in the dusk as he tightened the cinch of his grey. He turned and offered his hand. 'It's been pleasant meeting you, Miz Cahill. I — I kinda wish it coulda been earlier.'

'You mean before I was married?' She held onto his strong grasp. 'That's not something you should say behind Jake's back.'

'No, I guess not. Forgive me. It's just

that I don't like the way he treats you. It ain't gentlemanly.'

'He's not so bad. He's angry about the horses, that's all.' She wriggled her fingers free and gave him a wistful smile. 'I've made my bed and I've got to lie in it. That's life.'

'Yeah, there's no altering things now, Miz Cahill. I cain't help liking you thassall, even if it is wrong to say so.'

'Call me Rose, if we ever meet again. There's no harm in us being good friends.'

'Sure, Rose. That's a swell name. The Texas Rose. My pals call me Chas.' For moments she thought he was going to be as bold as to try to kiss her, but he swung up onto his horse instead.

'So long, Cap'n Chas,' she smiled. 'Remember to call in for a meal if you're ever passing this way.'

'Maybe that ain't a good idea,' he said, his face thoughtful, before he touched his hat-brim, and turned away into the night.

Rose watched for a while, her

19

emotions in turmoil, watched the darkness and the night sky, listened to the eerie howl of a wolf. He was right. It would be best not to meet again. They had no future. She turned back into the cabin.

'What in hell's taken you so long?' Jake snarled.

2

The next evening, as the dying sun bled across the plain, Jake was putting the plough horses in the barn when they heard the thudding of hooves and, looking up, saw a rider coming towards them from out of the red haze. At first Rose thought it was the Ranger returned, and then she screamed, 'It's him!'

Jake, too, saw the wide sombrero of the man silhouetted against the sunset blaze, saw the rifle held at his shoulder as he rode. He bit his lip with fear, and ran to grab for his longarm Kentucky propped against the barn wall. But, as he did so, a shot cracked out, and he was spun in his tracks. He cried out as the ball penetrated his shoulder. The rider came charging on. He tossed the one-shot rifle in the air, caught it by its barrel, and swiped it at Jake as he ploughed past. There was a sound like the crack of a coconut as the stock hit his head, and Jake went down.

Rose stood, petrified, as Joaquin Terrazos spun his mustang back, and flashed a gold-toothed grin at her. 'I come for my *Caballos*,' he shouted. 'I no like the trade.'

Jake was on the ground struggling to get up, blood pouring like a red curtain down his face. His eyes peered wildly through as Terrazos leapt down and grabbed Rose by her dark-brown curls before she could escape. He pulled her into him and gritted out, 'I come for woman, too. *Hermosa*, eh? Beauti-fool! She fetch good price.'

'No!' Jake choked on the word as the Mexican pulled the long-barrelled revolver from his belt and aimed it at his chest.

'No!' Rose's scream was drowned by the explosion, and, as a puff of black powder smoke rolled, she stared, transfixed with horror: her husband fell back, shot through the heart.

'No!' she screamed again, as Terrazos's grip tightened in her hair and he dragged her by it into the house. He dragged her through the living-room, and threw her up against a wall of the bedroom. He released her hair and cuffed her, viciously, across the face, grinning evilly as his dark face closed upon her. She fought to escape his foul mouth, but there was little she could do against his fierce strength.

He forced his mouth upon hers — not a kiss, more a demented sucking and biting. Then stood back in triumph. 'How you like thiss, huh?' He gripped her dress and ripped it apart, then began to attack her pale breasts with the same demented teeth, sucking and biting. When he hurled her onto the bed, pulled apart his filthy leathers and leered at her, he looked like a crazed animal. Rose screwed up her eyes, bit into her lips, tried to blot it out . . .

★ ★ ★

23

She was torn in body, torn in soul, when, some time later, when he had finished eating and drinking whatever he fancied in the house, he forced her at gunpoint to mount one of the mustangs, and tied her ankles to the stirrups, her wrists before her with rawhide.

'No,' she pleaded. 'Please don't take me.'

'You wish I keel you, I leave you here?' He snarled a grin at her. 'We ride. We go find my *amigos*.' He kicked open the corral gate and herded the mustangs out. His rifle over his back, his revolver stuck in his belt, he cracked his bullwhip snaking over their backs to send them galloping out over the plain, and giving a wild cry — 'Hai-yayiee!' — he charged after them, dragging her mustang on a lead rein, Rose hanging to the saddlehorn of the prancing, kicking animal.

★ ★ ★

'Jessis Christ!' Captain Charles Dawson hissed the words through his teeth as he saw Jake Cahill lying supine in a dark pool of blood. A chill froze his spine when he found the cabin deserted. 'Damn fool that I am. Hadn't I an idea something like this might happen?' He looked at the rumpled bedclothes, picked up a piece of torn blue gingham dress from the floor. 'My God! Poor girl! At least, she's still alive.' He stared at the piece of dress and muttered, 'Maybe it would be better if she were dead.'

★ ★ ★

His hair, thick and unruly, had the black sheen of a raven's wing, and his face was thin and wolfish, the boy who lounged on a pile of logs in Fort Worth and watched the Texas Ranger ride in. He was no more than fourteen, but tall for his age, and handsome in a youthful way. 'Hey, Cap,' he called, springing up. 'You captain of the Rangers?'

'That's right,' Charles Dawson said, reining in his heavy grey, swinging down and hitching her to a post outside the officers' quarters. 'What do you want?'

'I want to be a Ranger. I want to join up.'

Dawson smiled as he saw the youth standing there in his ragged, dusty denims, sunbleached boots, one sole threatening to part company from the upper, and battered old hat. 'Come back in four or five years' time, son.'

'Why? I can ride and shoot good as any man.'

There was something feral about the youth, his hunched, nonchalant, yet tense air, as if he had been living in the woods or wilds for some time, which, indeed, he had, since running away from home. His dark eyes held Dawson's intently. 'Give me a try, Cap. I'm ready to be a Ranger.'

Dawson glanced at the scrubby moke with a rope halter the boy had by one hand. It had no saddle. 'Where you steal that?'

'I don't steal. It's mine.'

'And where in hell you come from?'

'Catfish Falls.'

'So where's Catfish Falls?'

'Village in the woods. East Texas.' He jerked his head backwards. 'Back yonder.'

'Well, I suggest you return there. We only recruit tried and experienced men.'

'How can I be tried and experienced iffen you don't gimme a chance?' the boy yelled, as Dawson flicked his fingers in salute to an armed guard, stepped up to the commanding officer's door and hammered. He wasn't listening. He had more important things on his mind.

'Come on in,' Colonel Jesse Frampton shouted, as Dawson did so, rattling the door to behind him. 'You're back early.'

'There's been trouble. Bad trouble.' He gave the commander a brief, concise account of what had happened to the Cahills. 'All my Rangers are out on assignments. There's no way I can reach them. I'd like you to give me a platoon of your troopers to go after her.'

Frampton stroked the curls of his bearded jaw, frowning. 'It's bad, sure 'nough. *Comanchero*, you reckon?'

'That's right, according to her description, Joachin Terrazos himself. What he was doing in this area on his own I ain't discovered. Probably just sniffing out the land. He cain't have got far, Colonel.'

'Poor girl.' The colonel sat behind his desk and stared at his hands. 'I met her once. A handsome, spirited creature, too good for Cahill, I thought. But no decent man's going to want her after the *Comancheros* have done with her.'

'That's as maybe.' Charles Dawson turned his head and steely gaze out of the window. 'That's why we need to get on his trail fast.'

'You've already wasted a day.'

'This ain't a one-man mission; I need support. If he reaches the Llanos Estacados there's a hell of a lot of hostiles and *hombres* of Terrazos's ilk lurking about.'

'I'm sorry, Chas, I can't help you. My orders are to hold the fort. I can't afford to go careering off on some wild goose chase.'

'A farmer's been murdered, his wife, a respectable white woman, kidnapped. Doesn't that mean anything to you?'

'Sure, it means something. I hate the thought of what will happen to her. But, it ain't unusual, Captain. Hundreds of white women have been snatched, and very few have been found alive. There's a vast wilderness out there, Captain, and the Comanches and *Comancheros* rule that land.'

'If we acted fast, without sitting here dithering, we might get her back. Come on, Colonel. This is a matter of life or death.'

'Haven't you heard? There's a war brewing up. It only takes one fool spark

29

to the gunpowder keg and the whole show will blow up. My orders are to hang onto this fort and defend it if any of you crazy Texans take it into your heads to join the Rebel cause.'

'Aw, you've no cause to worry. It's all hot air. The politicians will sort it out. No one's fool enough to go to war over a few slave-holdings.'

'Don't be so sure. Relax, Chas,' — Colonel Frampton eased his chair back and undid a button of his dark-blue uniform, pulling a drawer open — 'you look like you could do with a snort.'

He produced a bottle of bourbon and filled two glasses. 'You buried Jake?'

'Yep. Fed and watered his stock.' The Ranger put the glass to his lips, thoughtfully. 'Guess we'll have to inform their relatives.'

'We'll take care of that,' the colonel said, smacking his lips on the bourbon. 'Best Kentucky. Funny to think in a year or so you and I might be enemies expected to try to kill each other. That's the way it's going.'

'I'm more worried this moment about Rose Cahill.' Dawson grimaced as he tossed back the fiery liquor. 'Just give me half-a-dozen men, Jesse.'

'Can't be done, Chas. You're on your own. Hell, I've been in this territory a long while, right back to '38 when the Comanches raided the Parker ranch, one of the leading Texan families, and took little Mary Parker. She was nine then, and in spite of all the searching we ain't seen hide nor hair of her. If she's alive she'll be a grown woman now. If the Comanches have still got her she'll have a brood of half-breed children. Who would want her? Maybe it would be best if we forgot her. And the same goes for Rose Cahill.'

'I ain't giving up that easy.' The captain slammed the glass down and turned to the door. 'I'll go out on my own.'

'That's damn foolhardy, Chas. You'll be wasting your time and most likely your life . . . ' The colonel's words petered out for the Ranger had gone, the door slammed. He refilled his glass and shook his head. 'Wasting his time . . . '

★ ★ ★

'What's wrong, Cap? You look a bit het up.' The youngster was leaning on his scrubby yellow horse, which with its hairy fetlocks looked more carthorse. 'Where you goin'?'

'What's that to do with you?' the Ranger grunted, as he led his grey to the stables for a feed of corn. 'You still here? About time you was headin' back to your farm. They'll be wonderin' where you got to.'

'Aw, I've had enough of sodbustin', pushin' a plough, scythin' hay from dawn to dusk. I told 'em, my ma and daddy, I'm leavin' to join the Rangers. They tried to stop me but I was too quick for 'em. This is my hoss. My uncle give him me for my tenth birthday. He's all I own in the world.'

32

'And all you're ever likely to from the sound of it. My advice to you, boy, is go back, knuckle down. Ants in his pants never did a man no good.'

'Guess I was born under a wanderin' star.' The youth gave a wide white-toothed smile. 'I'm lookin' for adventure, Cap. I aim to go places. I don't plan to be stuck the rest of my life on no durn farm.'

As he fed his grey some corn the captain assessed the youth. He had a lean look about him. No, he didn't have the air of a sodbuster. Too wild. The captain had seen too many of his sort, drifters who got in bad company, became horse-thieves, rustlers, who ended their brief lives on the gallows. He had had to tie the knot of the noose around the neck himself on occasions.

'You can shoot, you say?' Chas Dawson pulled a Colt revolver from his leather holster. 'Ever tried one of these?'

The boy took the weapon, curiously, from him. 'No, can't say I have. It's a six-shooter, ain't it?'

'Uhuh, remodelled according to Captain Walker's specifications.'

'Captain Walker the Ranger? Gee, he's famous.'

'Yes, a fine man.' Dawson noted that the boy didn't waggle the gun around, foolishly and dangerously, like some might. He held it in his palm, waiting to be shown.

'We had a lot of trouble with early revolvers blowing up in men's hands,' the captain said, 'but these are mighty reliable mainly due to finer steel, better design.'

The youth studied the rampant colt, on its hind legs, kicking out, the trade mark stamped on the frame. 'Sam Colt? He invented the revolver, didn't he?'

'Not exactly. They got a pepperbox revolver in Venice made in 1500. But Colt was the first man to patent his design in this country. He turns them out at his factory at Hartford, Connecticut. It ain't so easy to come by one down south. But, I tell you, son, the

man who ain't got one wishes he had
— especially a Comanch'.'

The boy continued to balance the
heavy weapon on his palm and glanced
at the Ranger. 'I'd dearly love to have
one of my own.'

'Maybe one day you will. Let's see, I
can spare a couple of slugs. Let's see
how you'd cope.' He looked over at a
big-bellied soldier watching them, and
winked. 'OK if he takes a pot at your
flagpole?'

'Go ahead.' The sergeant grinned
broadly for the pole was fifty paces
away and posed no danger to men or
animals. 'He ain't got a hope in hell of
hitting it.'

The youth flicked his hair out of his
eyes, and with a serious, determined
look on his face, took up position,
bracing himself, supporting his
extended arm by the wrist, cocking
the pistol with his thumb, squinting
along the sights. The gun kicked in
his hand as he fired. The explosion
cracked out, black powder smoke

billowed, and chips flew from the side of the post.

'Hmm?' he murmured. 'Maybe if I try with my left.'

This time he gripped the walnut butt in his left hand and used his right arm as a rest for the nine-inch barrel. He carefully cocked and squeezed and chips flew from the other side of the post. 'Hot damn! Nearly! It's got a kick like a mule on it.'

'What in Sam Hill's going on?' the colonel burst from his office. 'What you think this is, a shooting range?'

'What's the matter, Jesse?' Dawson smiled. 'You think the war's started? Just giving the kid a try with my forty-five.'

'It's durn heavy to hold up without wavering,' the boy said, looking somewhat crestfallen for he thought he had failed his test. 'Can I have another try?'

'No, you can't. Lead's too precious.' The Ranger held out his hand for the revolver. 'This weapon weighs three pounds. You need a strong wrist. And years of practice. You ambidextrous?'

'What's that?'

'He means,' the colonel explained, 'do you use both hands equally?'

'Yes, I do. Always have. Folks have remarked on it.'

'You surely not thinking of taking this lad with you on this foolish expedition?' Colonel Frampton demanded.

'Yes, I am. I need some back-up, Jesse. And you won't give me none. The boy's volunteered. He's old enough to join the army, so he's old enough to fight for the Rangers.'

'You mean you'll take me, Cap?' The youth's face lit up and he punched a fist in the air. 'Yee-hoo!'

Colonel Frampton frowned at him. 'Don't you realize, son, that if you go out into that godforsaken country you've got a ninety-nine per cent chance of not coming back?'

'Sounds OK to me. When do we start?'

'Just as soon as we've stocked up with some hard tack, beans, flour, coffee and jerky. Raise your right hand, boy, I'm gonna enrol you. What's your handle?'

'Peter Bowen.'

'Do you, Peter Bowen, solemnly swear before God and the colonel here to uphold the constitution of the newly formed state of Texas?'

'I sure do.'

'No need for the sure. Do you solemnly promise . . . '

When he was sworn in Dawson shook his hand. 'Welcome aboard. Pay's only five dollars a month, provide your own armaments, but ammunition can be claimed for. You get three cents a mile expenses in pursuance of a fugitive. The said fugitive must always be given the opportunity to surrender and be brought back for trial and hanging.' The captain grinned at him. 'There ain't many choose that option. Any questions?'

'No, suh.'

Dawson offered his hand to the colonel, and spoke in confidence. 'This kid's at a loose end, but I figure he's got good grit, and the makings of quite a shootist.'

'If he survives to his fifteenth birthday.'

'So long, Colonel. No hard feelings. Let's hope we don't meet again on opposing sides of the barricades.'

'Good luck, boys.' The colonel saluted and returned to his office. 'Keep your powder dry.'

Captain Dawson took a longarm rifle from the back of his saddle and tossed it to the youth. 'Can you handle this? A Kentucky. The best in the world, like their bourbon. Hand-crafted.'

'Whew!' The youth studied the silver engraving on the frame of a lady waving farewell to a Mississippi riverboat. 'I been shootin' squirrels and ducks since I was knee-high, but I never handled one like this. Where'd you get it?'

'It belonged to the man that Joaquin Terrazos murdered. He ain't got need of it no more. I guess his family won't object to our requisitioning it to go search for his wife, Rose Cahill.'

He led the way to the sutler's store. 'You're going to need a saddle, a blanket, rubberized poncho, tin mug and plate. And a hat. No Ranger rides without a decent hat. Try on one of them there. We'll dock the cost against your future pay.'

While the youth tried on some of the big hats piled on top of blankets and barrels in the gloomy store, Dawson asked the bald-headed man in charge, 'That consignment of Colts come in yet?'

'No. We're having difficulty gettin' 'em through. The government's already beginning to put a block on Colonel Colt's exports. Tell you what I have got, though, a seven-shooter.'

He reached under his counter and brought out a small nickel-plated revolver. 'The Smith & Wesson brothers' Model Number One chambered for their .22 cal rimfire. This year's state of the art. It marks a revolution in handgun history. The last one in the batch. I sold all the rest. They went like hotcakes.'

Captain Dawson weighed the short-barrelled lightweight handgun in his palm. 'Two-two? Ain't got the power of a peashooter.'

'You'd be surprised. That gun's worth its weight in silver.'

'How much?'

'Ten dollars. It would go for twenty south of the border.'

'Ten? Are you joking, man?' I'll give you seven.'

'Ten's the price. Take it or leave it.'

'Eight.'

'Done.'

'Add it to the bill.' Chas Dawson winced as he took a roll of greenbacks from his shirt pocket and began to peel them off. 'These bills ain't gonna be much use where we're going. But we're certainly gonna be in need of an extra revolver. Seven-shooter, you say?'

'Seven chambers in the cylinder. You leave one empty under the hammer for safety while you ride.'

'I generally rest mine between two chambers, but I guess it's a good idea. Got any slugs to fit?'

'Certainly, sir.' The sutler eagerly clawed in the greenbacks. 'One or two boxes? Dozen in a box.'

'Better make it six dozen. We might be away a while.'

'How do I look?' The youth had chosen a straight-brimmed, low-crowned black hat which he jerked down over his brow.

'Real purty,' the sutler crowed. 'That go on the bill?'

'Not the most suitable for the American desert but I guess,' Dawson sighed, 'the whims of youth must be allowed. Here, stick this in your belt, Pete.'

'Jeez!' The young Bowen stared at the revolver in his hand. 'For me?'

'You durn tootin',' Dawson grinned. 'Guess that's all we need. Seems like you've used up all your pay for the next six years or more.'

'Hang on,' the sutler said, producing

a leather belt and a sheath attached. 'This is the latest thang. You stick your gun in it, tie it steady round the thigh. Makes for an easy draw. Three dollars to you.'

'I'll take it,' the boy grinned, and notched the belt around his waist, stuck the revolver in, his long, delicate fingers flickering over the butt, trying the draw. 'Guess it could use some bear grease. Makes it easier. Or faster.' He shoved the revolver back in and proudly slapped it. 'I'm ready for action, Cap.'

'Hold your hosses,' Dawson said. 'I ain't done yet.'

'We got a nice line in ladies' doodahs.' The sutler grinned, knowingly. 'Just got 'em in for the officers' wives.' He held up a pair of frilled knee-length pantalettes attached by buttons to a camisole top, up against himself. 'Five dollars a set.'

'Gimme four of 'em. You got any necklaces, bracelets, bottles of perfume, anything cheap?'

'Sure.' The sutler laid out a handful

of beads and imitation pearls, cheap glass rings, embroidered purses. 'You can have the lot for ten dollars.'

'You goin' courtin', Cap?'

'Not exactly.' Dawson gave a brief smile as he stuffed his purchases in a canvas bag. 'Sling this over that carthorse of yourn. We may have to court a few Comanches along the way. This is the kinda stuff they like. OK *compadre*, let's get ready to ride.'

3

They went splashing across the wide-flowing Rio Brazos which meandered through red cliffs and cottonwood trees in tender green leaf. The girl hung onto the saddlehorn, her wrists and ankles red-raw and pained by every jolt, and her thighs, calves and backside aching from the days of constant riding. A black cloud of fear and apprehension hovered over her at the thought of what the future held, but short-term all she longed for was for darkness to arrive and the chance to rest her back. Her mouth was dry as dust and she envied the horses the few moments they were allowed to lap the clear river water. Terrazos had swung from his mustang and was squatted down filling his wooden canteen. He scooped up water in his sombrero and sloshed it over his head, shaking his greasy hair and giving a grin of bliss.

'Please,' she croaked. 'Can I — ?'

His expression froze, and he frowned at her, savagely. He rose in his tight leathers and held the sombrero up to her face, offering the delicious-looking water. But, as she reached her head forwards to try to get her tongue to it, he sadistically, slowly, drew it away. He offered it again, and took it back, teasing her, then gave a harsh laugh and tossed the water carelessly away. '*I* tell you what you have. You get nothin' 'less I say so. You understand?'

'Please,' she gasped, 'just a little drop.'

'Beg,' he smiled, a gold tooth flashing, the white scar vehement on his cheek. 'It good you beg. You know who boss, hay?'

Rose licked her parched lips and jutted her chin, defiantly, as salt tears trickled from her eyes. 'Why are you so horrible?' she whispered. 'You want me to stay alive, don't you?'

'Sure, you stay 'live. I get good price for you.'

With a clatter of spurs he leapt back on his powerful mustang, jerked the creature back on its hind-legs, hauling it around. He peered beneath his sombrero back in the direction they had come. '*Vamos!*' he screamed, grinding vicious rowels into the mustang's sides, and he set off along the river-bank, driving the herd, dragging the girl's horse by the leading rein.

Terrazos seemed in a great hurry to get wherever he was going. He was obviously wary of pursuit, pounding on and on, putting, she guessed, at least forty miles a day beneath their hooves. Whenever they had arrived at signs of habitation, a ranch house or settler's cabin, few and far between, he had cracked and slashed his whip across the backs of his herd of mustangs and sent them galloping on.

Perhaps he was fearful of the cavalry catching up? Suddenly a spurt of hope filled Rose's thoughts. Yes, Colonel

Jesse Frampton was an honourable man. He would not let this desperado kill a farmer, steal his wife and get away scot free. This was the United States. The cavalry would soon be on their tail. Was there any way, she wondered, she could slow the Mexican down?

But on and on they went throughout the afternoon, and by nightfall Rose was so weak with thirst she had slumped forward over the horse's neck and was being jolted up and down like a sack of flour.

When he cut her bonds from her ankles she could hardly get her feet from the stirrups, and tumbled to the ground. The impact knocked what breath she had left from her. When she tried to rise she toppled helplessly down again. The Mexican gave a mocking laugh, hauled her up and dragged her over to the shelter of a cliff overhang. He cut her wrists free and she gasped and stretched her fingers, took tentative steps to get her blood circulating again. They had been following the higher reaches of the river and, as the moon rose, its surface shimmered and coiled in whirls as it flowed by. Rose made a stumbling run towards it and fell headlong dipping her face and hair in the flowing stream, fearful he might drag her out before she could drink her fill.

But she heard only his sneering laugh, and eventually turned to see him squatted over a pile of dry sticks lighting a fire. She clenched a stone in her hand and wondered if she could not creep up and stun him. But she knew he was too crafty for her, too dangerous, and she feared his whip, his temper. She let the smooth rock fall from her fingers and staggered towards the horses which he had hitched to a running rope. Perhaps she could climb on one, make her escape? But a sense of hopelessness told her she would only get a short way before he caught up. Maybe it would be best just to throw herself in the river and drown? But, although she dreaded with horror the prospect of what might be in store for her at the hands of Comanches or *Comancheros*, the urgent spark of life, and her religious upbringing forbade her to do that. She would cling on to faint hope.

At least he gave her food, trout he had caught with his hands in the river, and a piece of fresh-baked *tortilla*. She nibbled at it, swallowing with difficulty, her mouth dry with fear of what he might do to her as soon as he was rested. But, when he crawled round to her, he contented himself with lasciviously licking her cheek and squeezing her to him.

'Haaagh,' he croaked, 'I got to keep you good. I get *muchos pesos* for you. Maybe I sell you in New Mexico to a rich *haciendado*? Maybe I trade you with Comanche?' He tossed her hair contemptuously 'Pity you no blonde. They get big price. But you, no bad. No — no bad.'

He bound her hand and foot again, and went sidling off, his rifle in hand, up among the rocks and trees. She knew he was going to keep a watch-out. Yes, he *was* worried about pursuit.

Perhaps, she thought, as she stretched out, drifted into sleep, he was not going to rape her again. Perhaps he did not want her to become pregnant, that she would be more valuable to him in a girlish state. It was strange that she had not had a child by her husband, but she had heard that it was sometimes years before a woman conceived. Any such hopes, and her sleep, were shattered when the Mexican scrambled back down and rudely awoke her. He leered at her, excited and intent on having fun. She discovered that there were alternative ways for brutish men to take their pleasure. She had never dreamed a man could so disgust her. But, with his revolver cocked and pressed to her temple, although she nearly choked with revulsion at her task, she could not dare resist.

★ ★ ★

51

Terrazos was trying to fool them, guiding his stolen, half-broken mustangs along through the shallows of the Brazos, criss-crossing from side to side. But Captain Dawson pressed on, and occasionally would come across deep tracks in the soft sand. The trail was easy enough to follow. He leaned from his saddle to study the prints. 'He's still a good day's ride up ahead. He's riding hard.'

'How you figure that, Cap?'

'Them shoe-prints are almost set firm by the sun. There's a deer track pressed down on top of them. the animals obviously use this pool to drink. I figure they passed through here early dawn. You get to know these things.'

'Yeah?' The lanky youth, his long legs around the wide back of his thick-waisted pony, tossed his black hair from his eyes. He had watched the ways of the quiet-voiced captain, nothing his careful stealth if they approached a hillock of rocks, the way he loosened his

.52 calibre Sharps carbine in the boot. 'If he's so far ahead why you so wary? You worried about *ambuscade?*'

'In this country man's got to have eyes in the back of his head. There's allus the possibility he'll leave the girl and the stock and circle back if he's an idea we're following. An' he ain't the only varmint skulking about the higher reaches of this river. You don't get much warning of an arrow 'til it's stuck in you.'

It was twilight by then, and with only a sliver of moon in the sky would soon be too dark to go further. 'We'll make camp here. Here's your chance to show me how you can handle that Kentucky. I fancy a taste of fresh meat. Man can have too much hard jerky.'

They hid in the rocks and watched the pool and, as the shadows lengthened, a small herd of white-tail deer came nosing down to drink, a big six-pronger buck leading his harem of does and young. The buck's regal head was held high, his nose and ears quivering, sensing danger. Dawson glanced at the youth, who was carefully raising the long-barrelled rifle, pulling it into his shoulder. 'Take the small doe,' he hissed.

He noted, with approval, the way Pete let them drink, taking his time, intent on getting a clean shot, lining his sights up on a spot behind the foreleg of the small doe when she was clear of the others. He wanted to make a heart shot. And he did. As the explosion of the longarm boomed out, almost simultaneously she fell. The others bent their knees, poised for seconds, looking about them in terror, before, almost as one, they went leaping away behind the buck, away through the rocks back into the darkness.

The youth darted down to examine his kill, pulling his bone-handled hunting knife to dispatch the gentle creature, but there was no need. She was dead enough. 'I'd liked to have got that six-pronger as a trophy,' he grinned, 'but I s'pose he'd be too heavy to carry.'

'That was a fine shot in this half-light. You know how to skin her?'

'Sure, Cap.' Pete deftly knotted a rope around her hind hooves and hung her from a branch of a nearby cottonwood tree. Then, with a few swift strokes, he slit her belly, extricated her intestines, tossed them behind a rock, and eased her coat off. 'Sorry about this, gal,' he said. 'Seems a shame to throw your hide away.'

'We're not carrying any excess baggage,' Dawson remarked, but approving of the youth's frugality, and his expert use of the knife. 'I'll get a fire made.'

When they had feasted on the roasted deer, Dawson sat back against his saddle with a tin mug of coffee, his blanket around his shoulders against the night chill. A cold mist had crept up along the river. 'I expect you think that was a fool thing to do, advertise our presence?'

'Man has to take a chance if he's gonna have his belly full, eh, Cap?

Anyhows, I guess whoever it is we're after's way ahead by now.'

'Whoever it is we're after's one of the meanest lowdown sidewinders, Mex, Indian or white that ever roamed this land, and that's saying something, boy. We ain't takin' no chances. If he comes back we'll be ready for him. You take first watch. Wake me at midnight.'

'How do I know when it's midnight?'

'You see those stars?'

'Yeah, the Big Dipper.'

'You'll see 'em move through the sky. Well, it's us who's moving, of course. But when they get to about there' — he pointed a finger — 'top of that ridge, hanging directly above, that'll be about time.'

'Funny, ain't it, all them stars up there. You reckon there's anythang beyond? You know, that Heaven they talk about?'

The Ranger gave a snort of laughter as he tossed away the dregs of his cup. 'Maybe, maybe not. But I kinda doubt it, myself. I figure this life can be either

Heaven or Hell, depending on what men make it. Unfortunately, most seem bent on creatin' merry Hell.'

'Yeah, funny ain't it, how sinnin's much more fun than Bible-punchin'? My ma says that's the Devil's ruse.'

'What the hell a boy like you know about sinnin'?'

'Aw,' Pete grinned. 'I may be only fourteen but I've had my moments.'

'There's sinnin' and there's sinnin'. There's good and there's evil. You got a choice. That you'll soon find out. But right now you ain't got time to sit stargazing and philosophizing. It's time you got that longarm cleaned and reloaded. That's a mark against you. You shoulda done that straight away.'

'But you told me to skin the deer.'

'You should have done that first without bein' told. Out here a ready-loaded weapon's the only way to survive. That barrel'll be getting gummed up.'

He watched as the youth did as he was bid, cleaning the barrel with the ramrod, pouring in a new measure of powder from his horn, taking a cone-shaped slug from his ammunition pouch, wrapping it in a greasy felt patch from the hatch in the rifle butt, and ramming both home. Pete's thin, handsome face was serious as he primed the frizzen pan and checked the flint was held firm, working quickly and knowledgeably. His long sensitive fingers handled the fine old gun with a kind of reverence. Here was a youth who already had a strange affinity with firearms.

'How about that?' Pete said, raising the longarm to his shoulder and squinting out into the darkness. 'With this I could knock out a buff' at five hundred yards, I bet.'

'Very good, soldier.' Indeed, the captain had rarely seen a trained trooper reload in so short a space of time. 'While we're at it I better show you how we reload these revolvers.'

They were like miracle shooting-sticks to the Comanches, and many had already been stopped in their tracks by the surprise of six bullets instead of one. But, once the six were spent, it was a long-winded business to get loaded again.

The captain took what he called a 'chargie' from his ammunition pouch, a grease-paper roll of powder, and slug. 'You snap off a round of percussion caps, see? Always remember to blow any oil or dirt out of the nipples. You see this lever under the barrel, you have to pull it down. Its purpose is to wedge the slug tight into the chamber. It effects what they call a hermetic seal. You can ride through a river and it will still fire.'

'Hermetic?' The youth watched, intently. 'Why you putting the hammer on half-cock?'

'That allows the cylinder to turn in one direction freely. You hold the muzzle erect, like this, place your chargie and ball in the mouth of the chamber.'

Dawson pressed the lever back tight.

'There we are, loaded. There's one empty chamber left. You want to try?'

He watched, gently advising, as the youth did so. 'You didn't let the hammer back,' he said, as it was returned to him.

'Well, I guess we're ready for whoever comes at us,' Pete said, checking his own revolver.

'As ready as we'll ever be. So, I think that's enough arms drill for tonight. You take your blanket and longarm and get up in the rocks. I'm gonna get some shut-eye.' The Ranger rolled over, his back to the fire, his Sharps carbine snuggled between his leather-clad knees. 'Goodnight, Pete.'

'G'night, Cap.' The youth got to his feet and paused, looking down at the man. 'Don't worry, we'll catch up with 'em. I'm sure we will.'

★　★　★

As dawn broke, Terrazos sighted a log cabin and corral of poles on a clearing of the river's bend. There was blue smoke trickling from a chimney. '*Hola!*' he hissed at her. 'Get back.' He turned his mustang and led her into the brush. He did not untie her bonds but hitched her mount tight to a tree bole. He glanced at her through narrowed eyes, removed his greasy bandanna from his neck, and, leaning over in the saddle, gagged her tight. 'You stay here. I got business to do,' he whispered, stroking her hair, mockingly.

Rose shuddered as he touched her, and was almost glad when he had gone if it weren't for the filthy tasting rag in her mouth, and the thought of what this bandit might do to whoever was in the cabin. What if there was another settler and his wife? Would he perform the same trick on them? She was left alone for he had herded the mustangs away with him. She waited, tensely, expecting to hear gunshots.

Terrazos, however, had, with his shrill yip-yip-yipping, as he sent the mustangs skittering before him, aroused the occupant of the cabin, who came running out, a rifle in his hands. He was a shiny-bald, skrimshanks of indeterminate age, scruffily dressed in 'puncher clothes. 'Hold it right there, stranger,' he called.

'*Buenas dias, señor*!' The sun's rays flashed on Terrazos's gold-toothed smile as he rode in, doffing his sombrero. 'My greetings to you.' He brought the string of horses in to a halt in a whinnying cloud of dust. 'Thees place . . . ees thees what they call way-station for stage line?'

'You got it.' The man did not take his rifle-aim off the chest of Terrazos. 'The Butterfield Overland Mail. What's your business, mister? You wanna buy a ticket?'

'No, meester. No ticket.' Terrazos laughed at the absurdity of the idea. 'The famous Butterfield Mail, eh? I have heard of you. Your stage-coaches, is it true, they go all the way across America to Los Angeles?'

'True enough. And on up to 'Frisco.

That's us. Transcontinental. Injins, weather, nuthin' stops the mail from gettin' through.'

'So, you must be needing many fine horses?'

'We git through quite a few. And you jest remove that hat from over that revolver you're wearing. Put it back on your head, show your hands where I can see 'em.'

'Oh, señor, why you not trust me?' Terrazos grinned and replaced his sombrero. 'I am honest horse-dealer.'

'There ain't no such thing. Nor any durn greaser I would trust, either. Why? You got that horse-flesh for sale?'

'Si. Thees my papa's fine stock. He sent me north of the Rio Grande to sell. You geev me good price, meester?'

'Yeah? Maybe I will. We been bad hit by the epizootic disease. Could do with more stock.' The stage-line ostler edged closer, took a look at the mustangs. 'Yes, not bad condition. This your daddy's brand?'

'Si, my daddy. He wait on death-bed

for my return. We poor, but we honest, señor. Take my horses, he say to me, take my fine *caballos* and sell to gringo. He geev you good price.'

'Yeah? You can save me the sob story. Ten dollars a hoss. That's the price. Stage'll be comin' through soon. You got here just in time. Put 'em in the corral.'

The baldy backed away into the cabin, his rifle still covering the Mexican. He hastily found a tin box buried in the dust floor, counted out some crumpled greenbacks, and returned to the yard. He waggled the rifle at the Mex. 'Git back on your hoss and vamoose.' He watched as Terrazos swung into the saddle, and tossed him the wad. 'Here's your cash.'

'*Gracias, señor.*' Terrazos counted the roll, and his smile gleamed like the silver studs of his bridle and saddle, the cruel spurs on his boots. '*Adios*, meester. Maybe I come back another day. *Andale*!'

The stage ostler watched him go

haring away. 'Yeah, go, you varmint. I ain't stayed alive fifty years in this wilderness by trustin' nobody. Still,' he sighed, lowering his rifle, 'I guess he was the answer to our prayer.'

4

The six-horse Concorde coach forded the Rio Brazos and went whip-cracking away as the two Texas Rangers came in sight of the way-station. 'Where 'n hail's that goin'?' Pete cried.

'San Francisco. You buy a hundred-dollar ticket in St Louis on the Mississippi and you'll be there in twenty-four days,' Captain Dawson said. 'Ain't you heard? It's been in operation since last year, carries the US mail.'

'Whoo!' The youth sat his horse and gazed after it as it disappeared in a cloud of dust heading across south-west Texas. 'I'd sure like to make that trip.'

'Yeah? Nearly three thousand miles of the worst road ever existed, through New Mexico and Arizona to California. Truly amazing. Makes our little journey seem like a picnic, don't it, Pete?'

'It sure does. But I got the feeling it ain't gonna be.'

A bald-headed ostler was leaning on a corral pole, his rifle in his hands. 'What you boys want?' he called.

'We're Rangers.' Dawson pulled his fringed buck-skin jacket aside to show his badge. 'You can lay that rifle aside.'

'I never lay my rifle down 'til I'm sure of a man, not even in my sleep. But it's OK, you can step down. If you was aimin' to catch the coach you're too late, it's gawn.'

'It ain't a coach we're looking for, it's a man.' Dawson's gaze wandered over the mustangs in the corral. 'Where'd you get those hosses? Them with that Diamond O brand? They're stolen.'

'No? Hot damn! I knew there was somethun' about that fella I didn't like. I paid him ten dollars a head in greenbacks. He swore they were his. Gave me some bull about his daddy was dyin' and they were sore in need of the cash.'

'A white scar across one cheek?'

'Thass right.'

'You're lucky to be alive.'

'Aw, I kept him covered all the time. I didn't like the looks of that varmint.'

'Yeah?' Dawson swung down and loosened the double-cinch of his saddle. 'If he had wanted to kill you I doubt you would have had much choice. That rattlesnake's like greased lightning on the draw.'

'I kidded him the stage was due to arrive, so I guess that made him think twice about any of them tricks.'

'When was this?'

'Early s'marnin'.'

'Those all the stock he sold you?'

'If you're lookin' to take 'em all back you'd better chase after that stage. There's six in the shafts.'

'No, your company will have to sort it out with the Diamond O boss. We're after the man. Did he have a young woman along?'

'Young woman? I ain't fed my eyes on a young woman in a month of Sundays 'cept for a coupla Comanche

68

squaws. Why? He stole her?'

'Yes.' Dawson nodded, his grey eyes serious, as he removed his hat. 'I'm afraid so.'

'Ransom on her?'

'Not as far as I know. I ain't been in touch with her family. Her husband's dead.'

'So why you going after her?' the baldicoot hollered.

Dawson sighed. 'Because us Texans don't like *Comancheros* taking our women, thass why. You had trouble with the Comanches around here?'

'Nope. There's the occasional wandering band but they mostly want to trade for coffee and sugar.' He gave a high-pitched cackle and stroked his sunburned skull. 'My scalp wouldn't be much of a trophy to 'em.'

'What do they trade with, stolen horses?'

'How should I know whether they're stole? If they got hoss-flesh to offer we're in the market for it. This stageline needs more than a thousand horses a year, not counting about five hundred mules, to keep going. How you think we git to San Francisco?'

'An' how you think the Comanch' get the hosses? By robbin' and killin' Texan settlers on the frontier. And I can tell you, mister, we are gettin' mighty tired of it. Anybody else receiving stolen property's liable to get strung up.'

'Aw, it ain't my fault. You got a gripe you better take it up with the government. They're the ones paying Butterfield six hundred thousand a year.'

'A vicious circle, you could say.' Dawson bent down to examine the forehoof of his mount. 'I got a loose shoe here. Can you fix it?'

'Sure, there's coffee on the stove. Help yourselves.'

They entered the welcome shade of the shack and did so squatting down, because there were no chairs, only a bed of skins. 'What do you think, Cap?'

'I think he senses we're after him. That's why he sold the broncs. They were slowing him down.'

'What about the girl? Do you think — ?'

'No, he just left her among the trees while he rode in here.' Charles Dawson winced, visibly, as if the coffee was too hot. But it wasn't the coffee. It was the image of Rose suddenly returning to him, the thought of how she must be suffering, the distasteful flash of imagination of what Terrazos might be doing to her. No, he did not think he would kill her, but a man like Terrazos might go too far. He spat in the dust, a sickened feeling in his stomach. Who, as Colonel Frampton said, would want her now? And, perhaps, the worst was yet to happen to her — if they did not catch up soon. If she were traded with the Comanche, or . . . it did not bear thinking about.

'Come on,' he said, springing up. 'He should have finished that shoe.'

Young Pete Bowen eyed him, curiously. Sometimes it seemed, by the captain's grim, moody look, that this was not just the case of a missing wife, that the loss of Rose Cahill meant more to him than that.

★ ★ ★

They pressed their horses hard for many days and several hundred miles following the upper reaches of the Brazos, taking the south fork, Captain Dawson needing all his sharp-eyed skills to follow a barely perceptible trail. It was time-consuming work, casting back and forth, seeking a broken twig, a dislodged stone, or, if they were lucky, an occasional clear hoof-print, and they would sometimes be rewarded by coming upon a camp-fire, the ashes cold, but not too old. A scrap of torn calico dress, signs in the dust as if of a struggle, cut like an icicle into Dawson's heart, and he spurred his mount on faster.

Gradually they were climbing into the Llanos Estacados, a steep escarpment rising to a vast step of level land which runs north and south across most of Western Texas. Those high plains, gashed by ravines, had, as yet, been little explored by white Texans, but they had long been the stronghold of Comanche and Kiowa tribes, and the haunt of Spanish traders from across the neighbouring border of New Mexico — the *Comancheros*.

They passed through Double Mountain Fork and, in the bakehouse heat of summer, it was eerily quiet. They were entering deep into enemy territory, and neither rider spoke much, both having a sense of eyes watching them. The sharp howl of a mountain lion away up in the rocks made them both, instinctively, pull in their broncs, and look around them, their faces tense as they heard an answering call. Lion? Or Comanche? Anybody's guess. Whatever, whoever, Dawson pulled the Sharps carbine from his saddle boot and carried it in readiness in one hand as he rode forward again, and Pete loosened the Smith & Wesson in his holster.

They were halfway up a narrow *arroyo* when the captain pulled in his horse and sat in the saddle his shoulders tense, slowly raising the carbine and cocking the side-hammer.

'You seen 'em?' he hissed.

'No.' The boy swivelled his neck, eyes searching. 'Where?'

'Up behind them rocks. Draw your sidearm. Slowly. Don't do anything to startle 'em. Cock it. Don't shoot unless I say so.'

There was a movement up on the rocky crest and Pete saw a warrior on horseback move into view against the dazzle of the westering sun. 'I see him,' he whispered, his mouth suddenly dry with fear. 'How many are there?'

'A fair bunch. They've got the drop on us, sure enough.'

And, sure enough, other warriors showed themselves, sitting their horses, silhouetted against the brightness. They were lean, nearly naked, except for skin loincloths and high moccasin boots that guarded against the thorns. They had lances, or long bows in their hands, decorated with feathers or scalps, which, like their plaited hair, fluttered in the breeze of the high ground. One had an ancient musket which was pointed threateningly in their direction. This scrawny fellow wore a straw pillbox hat, and shouted down at them harsh words that sounded like a raven's call. '*Quo! Quo! Krack!*'

'What's he want?'

'That's anybody's guess. Maybe our scalps. Maybe to take us alive. Get ready to jump down behind the rocks if they start anything. I'll go for the one with the gun. You take your pick of the others. I don't know about you, but I ain't in the mood to be slowly tortured by these lousy savages. I would rather die than let 'em have their fun. The end would be the same only it would take longer.'

Pete took a deep breath, ready to fight, too, rather than suffer that alternative. He raised the revolver to head height and gently but firmly thumbed the hammer. 'You speak their lingo, Cap?'

'A few words. Different tribes got different language. Sign is easier. They all understand that.'

The Comanche with the gun was shouting down at them, his face contorted into a kind of frenzy, words that were obviously threatening. The Texas Ranger shouted back up at him. 'Trade?' He beckoned him forward with his free hand, keeping the carbine tight into his shoulder, and made an open-palmed sign of friendship. The Comanches, for reply, raised their lances for throwing, and drew back the strings of their arrow-ready bows. Their leader cried out sharply to them to stay where they were, or so it seemed, for he carefully manoeuvred his horse down through the dust and rocks on his own, guiding it with his bare knees, his longarm, too, primed and ready.

'He sure is one ugly bastard,' Dawson said, as the Indian drew near. 'I'm gonna keep him covered. You get ready to holster your S & W and feel in them saddle sacks for a few trinkets. Not too much. We ain't gonna give 'em everything we got.'

The Comanche walked his pony slowly towards them now he had reached the *arroyo*, his narrow eyes above high cheekbones glimmering darkly as he peered along the longarm sights. His teeth appeared to be too large for his mouth, the broken front ones jutting through his lips. It gave the uncanny impression of his having a permanent crooked grin. Perhaps he was just looking forward to the pleasure of tieing them down over an ant hill, or other tricks.

'We come into your land because we are looking for a white girl.' Unwilling to lower his Sharps the captain tried to make one-handed sign language, accompanied by what words he knew. He gave the expressive wavering sign for woman, touching his chest to show she was white, and zig-zagging a scar across his cheek. '*Mexicano*. Joaquin

Terrazos. He stole her from us. We want her back.'

The Comanche really did grin at that. Why, he appeared to wonder, should anyone risk their life for some squaw? He touched his head as if all Texans were crazy, and called back up to his men. They, too, began to laugh, as if this was a great joke.

Whether their taunting laughter was infectious or what, but the captain smiled too, without lowering the Sharps. 'Pete,' he called. 'Holster your gun and start digging. Slowly now. Calmly and carefully. Get some stuff out.' He, himself, pulled a plug of chewing tobacco from his shirt pocket and offered it to the Indian, tossing it to him. The Comanche knew its purpose for he caught it and bit off a chaw, his cheek swelling.

Dawson indicated that he had other gifts and the boy reached back and hoisted the gunny sack from behind the saddle, carefully opening it and reaching inside. He found a necklace of imitation pearls and showed it, throwing it to the Comanche, who caught it on the barrel of his rifle. Reluctantly, he leaned the longarm across his dark, muscled thighs, and put the necklace around his throat along with his own thonged amulet and other wampum. He grinned again, made a croaking sound, and pointed to the Sharps.

'The greedy bastard's got his eyes on my gun.' Dawson shook his head. 'No way am I parting with this.' He tapped the walnut stock and gritted out, 'Gun for Terrazos. To kill him with. I kill him. I take the woman. And we go. You got any ideas where they are?'

The Comanche again pointed at the carbine, vehemently shouting out his words. Indeed, he seemed incapable of speaking in a modulated tone. Just as firmly Dawson waved his open palm from side to side and shouted, 'No. Where is she, you goddam heathen? Which way they headed?'

The rest of the band suddenly

seemed to think they were missing out on the goodies and rode their horses down the *arroyo*, giving wild, blood-curdling yips and excited cries as they did so. However, there was not room for them to go other than single file and they crowded in behind their leader. Some had a couple of feathers dangling from their hair, but most were bare-headed. They did not go in much for decoration, these fellows.

Pete looked at their harsh, gloating faces as they shouted out at him, and stretched forth open hands. He swung a leg forward over his bronc's neck and jumped lightly to the ground, dipping into the sack, and grinning as he produced a pair of lady's pantalettes. He squeezed past the chief and handed them to one of the warriors, who put them on his head, looking pleased with himself, if ridiculous.

Bracelets, necklaces, embroidered cotton bodices, tobacco, cheap brooches . . . he produced a bottle of perfume which one of the warriors uncorked and took a mouthful, screwing up his face and spitting it out.

'No, not like that.' Pete demonstrated, sniffing at it, dabbing it behind his ears. 'It ain't liquor. It's perfoom. You give it to your squaw.'

'That's enough. Get back here.'

'Sure.' The tall youth edged back uneasily, looking up at the dark faces, the stone skull-crackers, flint tomahawks hanging from their belts. 'I think they all got somethang. OK, boys? You gonna let us pass now?'

'They ain't told us nuthin' yet. The white girl,' Dawson shouted, angrily, 'where will he take her?'

The older Comanche spat a gob of tobacco, but seemed unsatisfied with his necklace. He remained mute.

'Give me a bag of coffee beans.'

Pete found one, spilling a couple out on his palm and showing them. 'Cawfee,' he said. 'Real nice. You crush 'em.'

Dawson reached for the bag, held it up. 'The woman?'

Maybe it was the steady-nerved way he held the carbine pointed at the chief's chest, never wavering, or the steely glint in his eye, but the Comanche began to jabber, pointing back up the *arroyo*. He snatched the beans, screamed words, turned his horse, and urged his men back up to the ridge, beckoning with his rifle for the Texans to follow.

On the ridge he pointed his bare arm out at a haze of other ridges darkly razor-sharp against the setting sun, pointing away across the high plain. He turned to the captain, laying his longarm across his horse's neck, and, earnestly, tried to explain, making the form of a large circle with his open hands, and a waving river running into it. 'Comancheros!'

At that he and his mob of wild-looking warriors spun their horses, and went haring away across the boulder-strewn plateau, the hair of men, horses and scalps waving in the wind, until they disappeared into the dusk.

'Phew!' Pete gave a whistle of relief. 'That was a close one.'

'Yes.' Dawson slowly reholstered his carbine. 'I think they meant there's some kind of big canyon thataways where the Mexicans come to trade.'

'Them Comanch' won't be creeping back in the night to try to git us, will they, Cap?'

'No. They are people of their word once it's given. Honest in their own peculiar way. Anyway, they're scared of ghosts. They stick close to their fire at night. It's the dawn you have to fear.'

'I guess they coulda killed us, stolen everythang we got.'

'I guess they could. They got nuthin' 'gainst burning, killin' . . . rapin',' he said, softly. 'But with them a bargain's a bargain. Thank God! It's them heartless *Comancheros* who cause all the trouble. They're the ones you cain't trust.'

The boy eyed him, the grave look on his face, and again wondered if he were thinking of Rose Cahill. How on earth could they possibly rescue her? But, like the saying went, faint heart ne'er won fair lady. They could only try.

'Come on,' Chas Dawson said. 'Let's find a place to camp. I want to make an early start before dawn.'

5

The River of Tongues they called it: Rio Las Lenguas. Here gathered a hodge-podge of Indian tribes — Comanches, Kiowas, Lipans, and the like — babbling in a variety of dialects and jargons, bargaining with Spanish-speaking *Comancheros*, while their white captives pleaded for mercy in their own languages. The river ran into a canyon the *Comancheros* named Cañon de Las Lagrimas, the Canyon of Tears, for here were assembled captives taken from the ranches of Texas, mothers and children to be torn apart and scattered to widely separated Indian villages, or a few sold to the New Mexican traders. The captives were treated as callously as cattle. Abductions at this time had become a veritable industry. However, the misery and tragedy of the unfortunates was not un-noted: hence the name.

Joaquin Terrazos went loping on his spirited mustang, dragging the torn and terrified Rose Cahill behind him, tied to her horse. The canyon opened into a wide amphitheatre where there was good water and lush grass and where herds of stolen cattle and horses were milling, bellowing and whinnying. Terrazos was greeted with shrill cries by both Indians and *Comancheros* as he rode in for he was well-known by both. If not respected, he was at least feared for his cold-heart, his guile, and his murderous ability with knife and six-gun.

He weaved his way through the camp-fires of the various bands, the heavy-wheeled covered wagons of the traders, doffing his fingers and grinning, proudly, at some he knew, and drew up before a large tent, canvas draped over poles, somewhat like an Arab chieftain's. Alongside, corralled behind a thorn fence were horses and cattle and, in another compound, a

86

clutch of haggard women, in dust-soiled dresses, all with the same look of despair etched on their features. For moments, as her ropes were untied, Rose Cahill met their gaze and knew that she was one of their sisterhood.

The interior of the tent had a similar Arab feel, for, Rose saw as she was dragged inside, it was darkly sombre, cool, and richly carpeted. Three men were standing, and a couple of Mexican girls were sat before a raised bed on which lounged, like some potentate, an elderly man, his white hair hanging to his shoulders, his limbs clothed in a suit of black velvet, ornately decorated with silver thread and pearl buttons. This, she was to discover, was Don Alfredo de Onate, to whom all *Comancheros* paid heed or tribute.

Terrazos pushed her roughly before him. 'What do you think, Don Alfredo? *Hermosa*, eh? How much you give me?'

The older man eyed Rose quizzically, and with a certain distaste. 'She looks a little the worse for wear, Joaquin. What have you been doing to her?'

'Pah! That is only the dust of travel.' He spat on his gloved fist and rubbed it against her cheek. 'And a little sunburn.' He gripped her to him and pulled apart her already torn dress to reveal her breasts, cupping them in his hands. 'See the milk whiteness of these, the tenderness of the rosy nipples. She is worth at least one thousand dollars.' He gave a drawn-out growl of lecherous appreciation, and jerked up her chin. 'Eh? I bet you have rarely seen such a beauty.'

The way Don Alfredo's tongue flickered out to lick at his thin lips beneath his sharp prow of nose it was as if he were inclined to agree. 'You mean the Americanos have agreed to pay a thousand-dollar ransom?'

'No, I mean as a wife for a rich haciendado. She is modest, sweet, obedient, hardly touched. I have treated her well. This is no common chacha. She has breeding. She comes from good family. You can tell, eh?'

Don Alfredo took a cigar from a leather case and signalled to one of the girls to light it for him. He blew out smoke, watching it form a ring, and his eyes returned to Rose. 'Show me her legs.'

Terrazos pulled her dress high, revealing her nakedness.

'*Bueno*, eh?' He stroked her legs expressively, let the dress fall. Then he pulled her lips apart with his gloved fingers. 'See those teeth? The colour of her tongue? The sparkle of her eyes? The richness of her hair?'

Don Alfredo rattled out a question in Spanish at her, and translated into English. 'Are you single or married? Have you any children?'

'My husband is dead,' Rose said. 'He killed him.'

Don Alfredo smiled as the men cackled with laughter. 'I asked about children?'

'No.' She shook her head. 'None. I beg you, *señor*. You appear to be a gentleman. Return me to my family. I am sure they will pay a reward.'

Don Alfredo laughed this time. 'That would be too much trouble. Have no fear. We are not going to sell you to the Comanches, although I am sure they would offer many horses. No, regard me as a marriage broker. I am going to find a wealthy husband for you. We Mexicans appreciate a beautiful girl. He might be a little older than you would like, but most rich men are.'

Rose stared at him, her eyes troubled. 'The American Army will have sent out a column to look for me. Colonel Frampton was a friend of my husband's. You would be wise to return me to Fort Worth. Otherwise you could be in bad trouble, *señor.*'

This, too, seemed to impress the men, dressed *vaquero*-style, in tight leathers and rowelled boots, armed to the teeth. Don Alfredo raised an inquisitive eyebrow at Terrazos, who growled, 'Nobody has followed me.'

'Are you sure?' Don Alfredo rapped out.

'Sure I'm sure. The gringos are withdrawing their soldiers to the north. They are getting ready to make war on each other. Nobody's interested in one missing girl.'

One of the girls filled a glass with wine and handed it to Don Alfredo, who supped at it like a connoisseur. Rose Cahill gave a swallow of her dry throat as she watched.

'Well, she is certainly too good to give to the Comanches, or to sell as brothel-fodder. I will give you five hundred. My top price.'

'Pah! I could get more if I put her up on the auction block.' Terrazos gripped her arm and began to steer her out of the tent.

'Terrazos!' Don Alfredo's voice snapped out. 'That would not be wise.'

Joaquin Terrazos froze, and slowly turned to face the three men standing with rifles raised, the deathly holes aimed at his heart. His hand moved for the butt of his revolver, but again he paused, his narrowed eyes glinting.

'Don Alfredo, this is not friendly.'

'Five hundred. Take it or leave it. Come, *amigo*' — he reached for a leather pouch from a nearby table — 'we do not want to argue with you.'

'In gold?'

'*Si.*'

'Very well.' Terrazos caught the gold as it was tossed to him. 'No doubt you will make twice this amount. But you have me at a disadvantage.' He thrust Rose forward. 'Have her.'

As Terrazos left the tent Don Alfredo chuckled. 'Or perhaps three times that much.' He flickered his fingers, disdainfully. 'Take her away, bathe her, dress her. Bring her to me here after dinner. I need to sample my wares. Now, let's take a look at those other creatures. Let's see how much the Comanches will give us.'

★   ★   ★

'Shoot to kill,' Captain Dawson said, as they took cover in the rocks on the edge of a ravine scarred across the grassland. 'Musket first and then your revolver.'

They had heard the groaning clamour of a herd of beeves, the sharp cries of riders driving them along, and glimpsed tossing horns, seven men in tall sombreros, through the dust cloud. Fortunately, they had not been seen and had managed to hide their horses behind the rim.

'You take the one riding point.' The Ranger tucked the Sharps carbine into his shoulder. 'I'll try to get the one at the rear. Then fire at will.'

Pete gritted his teeth as he rested the long barrel of the Kentucky on a rock. He was not sure he liked this. He had never fired at a man before, fired to kill. 'Ain't this kinda unfair?' he muttered. 'Didn't we oughta challenge them, like you said. Give 'em a chance to surrender?'

'I ain't fond of bushwhacking, myself,' Dawson gritted out. 'But life ain't fair, sometimes. You can be sure them are rustled cows, Pete. And these men all murderous scum. It's the only way.'

Dawson did not wait for a reply, for the first man and the herd of seething cattle, about 300 head, were almost level with them. He squeezed out a .52 calibre slug. *Ker-ack*! And saw one of the riders in the rear catapult backwards off his mustang.

Pete hastily took aim, and blasted the point from his saddle. He stared, almost in disbelief, and a certain shock, as the Mexican lay on the ground and was trampled by hooves. He was dead.

But, if he did not keep his head down so would he be, too, for the riders were yelling and cursing, pulling out revolvers and lambasting them in reply. *Ker-pow*! A bullet glanced off his rock and singed his cheek. He lay the musket aside, snatched the Smith & Wesson from his holster, and sent two other men tumbling from their mustangs before his seven were spent.

With a rumble and a roar, the cattle set off stampeding along the narrow arroyo and a rider, who tried to slow them, screamed as his horse was gored and he was swept away. As the dust and gunsmoke settled it looked as if every one of the seven horsemen was dead.

'Good shootin', Pete,' Chas Dawson called, as he scrambled down warily to inspect their bodies. 'He's about your size. Get his clothes on.'

It felt mighty strange to Pete putting on dead man's clothes, pulling the tight velvet trousers up around his waist, the high-heeled boots and spurs, the flower-patterned shirt, a rather dandy snakeskin jacket and gloves. He decided to keep his own bandanna and Stetson, rather than put on a big sombrero. But he jerked a pair of leather shotgun chaps, silver conchos on their sides, from another of the corpses, and tried them on.

'How do I look, Cap?' he shouted, as he fixed his gun-belt, and reloaded.

'Grab one of those mustangs. We'll take your bronco as packhorse.' The captain, who, from not shaving, had a considerable stubble, was rubbing mud onto his face. 'No need for you to do this. You look kinda Mex, as it is.'

'Yeah,' Pete said. 'I think my granpappy had some Spanish blood. Or maybe Injin. I dunno.'

'Let's go catch them cows. They should be our passport to get into that canyon. That's where they musta been headed.'

★   ★   ★

Rose Cahill was dragged from Don Alfredo's tent by the two girls, an armed guard following, and taken to the nearby riverbank. They were younger than herself by a couple of years, but much older in knowledge of the world. Dark-eyed, mischievous creatures, their lithe limbs in loose, colourful dresses, shrilling incomprehensible Spanish, they tore her clothes from her until, in spite of her protests, she was naked, and plunged her into the water, washing and stroking her body with impudent hands. The guard sat on a rock and watched with interest the gleaming body of the new girl, white as a fish's underbelly. 'Don Alfredo gets all the luck,' he growled, as he rolled a *cigarillo* in a corn husk.

When they had sported in the water awhile, ducking her under to wash the grime from her hair, they pulled her out and threw a blanket around her shoulders, led her back to a canvas-covered *carreta*. She was forced to climb into the wagon and watched as the girls opened a trunk and pulled out dresses, underwear, baubles, bangles and beads, squabbling as to what would be most flattering for her. They tossed her short, lace-trimmed pantalettes, and, giggling, laced her into a striped basque, its tightness making her gasp, forcing her already rather prominent breasts high in its cups. They chose a flame satin dress, its ruffled skirt like a dancer's, its neckline low. In fact, a thoroughly indecent outfit. They combed out her damp hair until it was rilling luxuriantly across her brow, and down to her shoulders, and fitted silver, high-heeled slippers onto her feet. It would have been pleasant to feel clean and fresh again, if it had not been for the sickening sensation in her stomach, the thought that all this preparation had an awful purpose . . .

'You be nice to Don Alfredo,' one of the *señoritas* whispered. She gripped her head, while the other powdered her face, painted her lips, added a touch of rouge to her cheeks, and splashed perfume. 'An' he be good to you.'

There was a touch of cruelty about the high cheekbones, the cold eyes of the other girl who was doing her face. 'You no good to heem,' she muttered, 'he wheep you bad.'

'*El es un gran general,*' the other put in. '*Commandante de los Llanos Estacados*' — she swept her arm pointing westwards — '*y las montanas. El general* he like' — she made a motion of her coiled fingers and flickered her tongue. '*Comprende?*' she smiled.

'Eugh!' Rose swallowed her disgust. Was she expected to be the concubine of that old man? She had escaped from Terrazos, but..it was like out of the frying pan into the fire. By now, however, she had become immune to humiliation, almost accustomed to being a slave. She looked at her rope-burned wrists and ankles, and knew only relief not to be roped over a horse, not to be half-dead from exhaustion and thirst. At least, she was not to be thrown to the Comanches. She stared blankly at the girls and nodded. She had heard of Pawnee maidens who were chosen as blood sacrifices, who were dressed up, fêted, carried on palanquins, prior to death. She felt much in common with them, for she had given up all hope of rescue.

★ ★ ★

Chas Dawson and Pete managed to catch up, after a five-mile run, with the stampeded longhorns and slow them when they reached a stream. It meandered on towards the open mouth of a high-rocked canyon and it was not too difficult, after they had drunk their fill, to sent them ploughing and tossing on their way for they liked the scent of water and good grass.

'They've been brought a fair piece,' the Ranger drawled. 'That brand's a spread on the Wichita River. Them fellas didn't get these by lawful means. Well, here goes, boy. This looks like the canyon them Comanch' had in mind. We'll jest drive 'em in and play it by ear. Keep your fingers crossed.'

Although Dawson appeared relaxed as he rode back and forth herding the beeves along, Pete could tell by the tension on his face that that was not the case. 'Hey, Cap,' he called. 'If we find Miz Cahill how we gonna git her out?'

'If you come up with any ideas you jest let me know. You got any Spanish?'

'*Si, mucho*. I learn it from *mi buen amigo, Carlos*.'

Most Texans did, living side by side with the former inhabitants of the state before it was taken from them.

6

Ranger Dawson advised the boy from Catfish Falls to say as little as possible as they rode into the Cañon de Las Lagrimas for, however proficient their Spanish, it might be detected as not the genuine article. They drove the cattle into the canyon, and as they entered its sheer walls they experienced a sinister sensation of entering a trap they might not escape from.

'Here they come,' Dawson said, as he saw the clusters of skin tipis dotting the wide base of the ravine, and Comanche warriors running to leap onto ponies and join a gang of New Mexicans who had spotted them and were riding their mustangs out to meet them. He hoped they would not recognize the clothes and horses of *los hombres muerto*.

Dawson had his bandanna tied high against the dust, and paid little heed to the *Comancheros* who came alongside and shouted out to him, or indeed to the bunch of wild-looking Indians who charged out on their ponies to inspect the herd.

'*Buenas tardes, muchachos,*' Pete grinned, for the sun was sinking fiery gold behind the western hills and it would soon be dark, adding, in Spanish, 'You want to buy cows? We come a long way. Where we take them?'

A Mexican, his bald head burned almost black by the sun, the remaining rats tails hanging down to his shoulders, a sombrero hanging on his back, and a thick leather belt tied around a striped *serape*, a pistol thrust in it, eyed him and the longhorns, malevolently, but beckoned him onwards with his thumb, and led the way through the Comanche encampments, to a loop of the river away from other milling herds of horses and cows. 'You two bring these by yourselves?' he demanded.

'Yes, why not?' Dawson replied in Spanish, lowering his bandanna. 'A lousy Wichita rancher murdered most of our men.'

'Yes,' Pete smiled. 'He did not like us taking his cows.'

'Maybe you get a better price you drive them onto New Mexico,' the man, who introduced himself as Miguel, told them.

'Maybe, but maybe we want to sell them now,' Dawson said.

'*Si*, we need *dineros* for whiskey, for *muchachas*.' Pete gave a whistle as he spotted a couple of Indian girls, bare-breasted, bathing in the river. 'Maybe we had enough of driving these cows.'

'You keep your hands off Comanche women or they skin you alive. I'm not joking, *amigo*. Maybe I take this herd off your hands. You no need to see Don Alfredo.'

'Who's he?'

'Him, he's the big cheese.' Miguel pointed to a large canvas tent pitched at the far end of the canyon. 'He always wants to take the cream.'

'You can have them,' Dawson said, and named a price. After some haggling one was agreed, and Miguel took a pouch from under his *serape*, paid him out in gold coin.

'*Gracias, señor,*' Dawson said, 'good doing business with you.' He gave a wink to Pete. 'Let's go take a look around.'

The hectic scene in the Cañon de las Lagrimas was nothing if not interesting to the Ranger, who pulled his sombrero, with its wide weighted brim, low down over his eyes. They led their horses through the milling crowd where all day brisk trade had been going on between *Comancheros* and Comanches. The men who had brought their wagons across the deep rutted trails from New Mexico had barrels of whiskey, blankets, trinkets and cheap geegaws to barter with the Indians for cattle on the hoof, horses and mules by the hundreds of thousands over the years, stolen from Texans. The Indians wanted to sell jerked buffalo meat in sacks, or buffalo robes, but the New Mexicans had lost interest in that, and many Comanches were still trying to get rid of such wares, hawking them about.

As for the Comanches, they were more keen to get hold of whiskey and guns. The two Texans gave a wide berth to some who already appeared to be three sheets to the wind, staggering about, whooping it up, fighting for possession of a whiskey keg. One fired off a musket, the ball whistling over their heads, and the Comanches began to fight for that. They reached a spot where other guns were being sold, or bartered, from the back of a wagon. The Ranger was glad to note that most were old-fashioned muzzle-loaders. Colt revolvers were in short supply, and he had heard of men paying as much as $100 to possess one out here in this No Man's Land. The Comanches would use the rifles mainly to hunt buffalo, easier than the old method of riding alongside and hurling a lance. Or, perhaps, for war.

It seemed like this gathering of the clans was held every other full moon in this canyon, so they had struck lucky. If lucky it could be deemed to be among warriors and hardened Mexicans who would tear them to pieces if they suspected their true identities.

The trade had been going on for so many years, it was so well established, that goods changed hands as naturally as in markets in more civilized parts of the continent. Dawson noted that the Comanches were nearly always woefully cheated. A bottle of whiskey bought a prime mule from an Indian. A packet of coffee was traded for a pack horse. As he already knew, stolen cattle did not fetch a good price here, but would be eagerly paid for in gold once they reached New Mexico. The Comanches appeared to be ready to dispose of whole herds for knives, axes, muskets, powder and ball.

'I reckon they'd give away their grannies for a bottle of whiskey,' he muttered to Pete. 'If anybody would want them.'

It was nearly dusk and suddenly there was a stirring at the far end of the canyon, and a general movement towards it. A tall, thin Mexican, with flowing white hair beneath his ornate, silver-hung sombrero, had come out of the big tent, accompanied by his bodyguard. He had strolled over to a corral of thorns, behind which, like caged beasts, ragged women were standing, or sat, heads bowed, in attitudes of despair. Some clutched children to them. The old *padrone* who, as he got close, Dawson assumed was the big shot of the place, Don Alfredo, had mounted a platform and pulled out a silver-engraved revolver, which he used as a gavel. Women and children were being dragged up beside him and bidding began. By the way they craned forwards, their eyes bulging, the half-naked Comanches obviously had a craving for a white squaw. They opened and clutched fingers to show how many horses or cattle they would bid.

It was dusk by this time, but a large bonfire splashed its light onto the greedy, eager faces as Don Alfredo banged his revolver butt on a post, and some farmer's wife was dragged, screaming and sobbing, away from her children. The Comanches appeared eager to buy the youngsters, too, and, if successful, would, with a yell of triumph, throw them over a horse's back and go riding off to their camp. Whether they would bring them up as their own, or offer them for ransom, Dawson was not sure. He felt numbed with anger and pity at the spectacle, frustrated by his helplessness. How could he help these poor women and children? It would be impossible to rescue them all. If he started shooting and tried to make a break with some of them, he doubted if they would get further than a mile. He tried to make a mental note of who they were for future rescue expeditions. He had come out to rescue Rose Cahill and it was for her he was waiting to bid if she was dragged up onto the auction block. Perhaps he ought to be ashamed that he was fixated on only one of the captives, and she the prettiest of the bunch; perhaps his own motives were not so noble, but it was her he wanted, and her he intended to get.

Most of the women were not exactly good-looking. Most were what is charitably defined as plain, not helped by their rags, and the hardships they had seen. In better circumstances most would be just raw-boned, wiry ranch women. But this did not deter the bidding. It rose highest for the more comely, with a bit of lard in the right places, but the whiteness of their skin seemed to be the deciding factor.

It was not only the Comanches who wanted them. There were stern-faced Mexicans in the crowd, who raised their snake whips and cried out bids, and yet another screaming female was dragged away, bound for the brothels of Mexico.

'Can't we do anything?' Pete hissed.

Dawson shrugged, helplessly. 'Like what?'

The last of about thirty victims had been thrown to their new slave-owners, and the *Comancheros* were busy collecting up the bartered cattle from the Comanches, and the Mexican whoremongers' gold. Don Alfredo's stately presence kept everything under control. Eventually he seemed satisfied that all debts had been paid and business transacted satisfactorily, and returned to his tent.

Dawson shook his head. 'She wasn't among them.'

'Who?' Pete asked, forgetting in the excitement of it all just who they were looking for.

'Rose.'

Again the youth sensed that this was not just Ranger business they were on. To Dawson this was a personal matter and one that obviously affected him. His face was grim as he turned to Pete. 'You keep the horses standing by and ready to ride,' he said. 'I'm going to try to get a look inside that tent. It may be our only chance.'

'Cap, you sure that's wise?'

'No. I ain't, but I'm gonna try it, anyhow. If anything happens to me don't try anything on your own. Skedaddle back to civilization, git your ass outa here.'

★   ★   ★

Rose Cahill had waited in trepidation in a smaller tent adjoining the bigger one. She had heard the screams of the women and children being sold, all the clamour of horses and cattle outside. She had listened to men's guttural voices as they entered the larger tent, the clink of bottles and glasses, had watched as trays of food were carried in. Eventually it went quiet as the men appeared to leave, shouting their goodbyes, and her heart began to thump harder.

'Come on, honey,' the girl called Juana whispered, and, gripping her wrist, led her into the main tent.

'*Hola!*' The gaunt, silver-maned old man was lying on his couch, clothed now in a long, embroidered kind of nightgown. A boy skivvy was busy collecting up the used plates and glasses, half-eaten food onto a tray, glancing furtively at her as she passed.

'Come and sit beside me,' Don Alfredo called, tapping a cushion below his couch. 'Come, don't be shy. You are hungry, aren't you?'

Juana led her over, while the other girl, Celeste, went to sit beside him, stroking his hair and fluttering kisses on his face. 'My, what a beautiful butterfly they have turned you into,' the old man quavered, as his eyes lingered on Rose's thrust-up pale bosom in the tight-waisted flame satin dress. 'Come, sit beside me.'

Rose did so, awkwardly, and started, like a spurred horse, when she felt his fingers touching her cheek. 'Please,' she said, 'don't do this.'

'Do what?' Alfredo asked. 'If you

want some supper you must sing for it. It is you who must do things to me.'

Rose glanced nervously in his direction and could not help noticing that something like a barber's pole was pressing out of Don Alfredo's nightgown. He might be old, but . . . she swallowed her surprise and fear.

'Give the girl a glass of wine. It might get her more in the mood.' He clapped his hands and spoke in Spanish, and Celeste passed her a brimming glass of white wine. Rose accepted and sipped, hesitantly. It was certainly refreshing, she thought. Maybe, if she got drunk, she would pass out, she would know nothing about this.

Don Alfredo clapped his hands again, and the two girls began to dance, clipping their fingers, swaying sinuously, spinning their skirts to reveal their bronzed legs and to show they were wearing nothing beneath the skirts. Suddenly they divested themselves of their dresses and rolled, laughingly, down on the cushions beside Rose. She watched, horrified, as they kissed and caressed each other's bodies, beginning slowly, sensually, and becoming more frantic, their hair flying about, fondling each other's breasts and more intimate parts.

'Aren't they sweet?' Don Alfredo remarked. 'My little darlings. Wouldn't you like to join them?'

'No.' Rose emptied the glass and shook her head. 'No, I wouldn't.'

'Bravo! Myself, I like a woman who is like a wine, best served chilled. Your coldness appeals to me.' Suddenly his fingers had grasped her skull, he had thrown apart his nightgown, and he was thrusting her face, as she resisted, into him. 'Come on, my beauty. You know you want to.'

What could she do? There were armed men guarding the doors. Wouldn't it be best to do it willingly, get it over with, than be forced to submit . . . ?

★ ★ ★

Chas Dawson strolled around the big tent as if he were just taking the night air. There were men standing at each of the door entries, fore and aft, and one on each side, armed with carbines and revolvers. Here goes, he thought, as he rolled himself a cigarette, paused beside the guard at the more darkened rear of the tent. Nearby, cooks were busy washing and clattering dishes. He patted his pockets, as if futilely seeking a match, then enquired of the man, 'Can you give me a light?'

The guard eyed him, viciously, but rested his carbine, and offered his own burning cigarette. Dawson bent to suck a light from him and, as it caught, brought his left fist up hard to connect with the man's stubbled chin. 'Agh!' the man coughed his surprise as the edge of Dawson's right hand chopped a blow to the side of his neck. He went down, out cold. Quickly, Dawson pulled him over into the darkness. He returned to the rear of the tent and dodged inside. He found himself in a smaller, tented compartment. It was empty. He listened and could hear, on the other side of the canvas, a murmur of voices, a rustling, a gasping and deep breathing, sounds of . . . what? He parted the canvas and put an eye to the gap and was struck dumb by what he saw . . . the old white-haired Mexican was naked on the cushions, his withered, scrawny body being tended by three females, two of them bare-assed naked, and one in a flame satin dress, hoicked up around her thighs, her face painted like a harlot, her breasts hanging free as she knelt and the old man fondled her. Was it.. could it be . . . Rose Cahill? Dawson could hardly believe it. For, what she was doing, she appeared to be doing willingly. The Ranger almost turned on his heel and left her to it. But, he could not do that. He stepped inside and, without them being aware of his tread across the thick carpets, put his revolver barrel to the back of the Mexican's head.

Rose Cahill, and the other girls,

looked up with equal surprise as the old *patron* froze.

'Chas?' Rose murmured, as if in a dream, drawing away from the old man's body. 'Chas Dawson? What are you doing here?'

'Surprised? I expect you are. Sorry to butt in on your fun, my sweet. But I've come to take you back.'

'I . . . ' she stuttered, blinking her eyes at him. 'I . . . ' She wanted to tell him that this was not her idea, that . . . but what was the use? She had been caught *in flagrante delicto*. Her face blushed scarlet as she tried to cover herself, rearrange her gaudy dress, 'I — really . . . ' There was nothing she could say for shame. How could this man she had been thinking of constantly, want her now? She was a degraded woman. A common whore.

'Come on,' he gritted out. 'Let's go. That's if you want to?'

Rose scrambled to her feet. 'Yes, I want to. How I want to. Thank God you are here. Oh, Charles, you must believe me, I had given up hope.'

'I am tempted to shoot this old dog, but I don't want to arouse the guards.' He raised the revolver and cracked it across Don Alfredo's skull. He left him slumped on the cushions, and put a finger to his lips to the two girls.

'Not a word.' They stared at him, their mouths open, and shook their heads.

He took Rose's hand, and led her out quickly through the rear flap. As he did so, one of the girls inside screamed. There was no time to get to Pete and the horses. He saw a mustang tethered nearby, unhitched it, and leapt into the saddle. He swung Rose up behind him and, touching his spurs, went pounding away. One of the guards ran out to stop him, his carbine raised, but Dawson's horse bowled him out of the way. Another *Comanchero* ran forward, aiming his rifle. Dawson got his revolver shot in first, spinning him in his tracks, and galloped on, Rose clinging on around his waist. She pressed her face against his back and for a few moments experienced an elation, an ecstatic joy . . . before it all came crashing down.

Pete was waiting with the three horses in the darkness 100 yards away and saw the Ranger with the woman behind him, swerving through camp-sites, leaping over a cart, as he came galloping towards him. 'What'n hell?' he said. He was about to jump on his own mustang, when he saw a man crouched by his camp-fire swing a pair of rocks attached to a rope. He sent the weapon spinning towards the charging horse. It wound around its forelegs, and, the next moment, the mustang was toppling into the dust, its passengers sent flying.

Before Chas Dawson, or Rose Cahill, could get their breath, or back on their feet, they were surrounded by *Comancheros*, and had lariats tightened around their throats and arms. Pete watched, in a lather of indecision. Should he start shooting, try to get them free? Or would that be suicidal?

He cocked his Smith & Wesson and then slowly released the hammer. No, it would be an impossible mission. There were too many of them. He had no chance.

He stood and watched as the Mexicans dragged their captives back to the tent, thrust them through its doorway, back to what, for Dawson, would surely be certain death. 'What'n hell am I gonna do?' he asked.

7

Don Alfredo fluttered his eyelids open, touched his head, and groaned, '*Nombre de Dios*! What hit me?'

'*He* did.' Juana bent over him as he lay on the cushions, and patted his brow with a damp cloth. She nodded towards Charles Dawson who was restrained by the rawhide noose strung tight back and tieing his wrists behind him. 'If I had not screamed out he would have escaped with her, *patron*.'

'Careful, *señor*,' One of his men helped him to his feet. 'He did not get far. Raoul brought him down with his bolas. Look what we found in his pocket.' He showed him the tin badge of a Texas Ranger. 'He is a gringo.'

'Ha!' Don Alfredo stood, unsteadily, arrogantly thrusting away support. He stared at Rose Cahill, who was similarly held by the guards with a rope around her throat. 'So, the noble Ranger thought he could rescue the lady? How amusing.'

He put a hand to the back of his head and looked, sourly, at the blood on his palm. He straightened his embroidered nightshirt and reached for a six-tailed quirt hung on a nail of one of the tent poles. Its handle was the hoof and leg of an antelope, the six short lashes of thinly woven leather knotted at their ends. He flicked it and approached the Ranger. 'What is your name?'

The Ranger's hat had been knocked from his head, and he tossed his wavy brown hair from his eyes and bluffed, without much hope of success. 'Captain Dawson, out of Fort Worth. I am the advance party of US Cavalry. If I do not ride out of this canyon within the hour with that woman they have orders to attack. To avoid any bloodshed you had best release us both immediately and I promise you will hear no more of this.'

Don Alfredo smiled, flicking the

quirt's tails across his wrist, stroking them out, lovingly. 'You lie. You think the Comanche would not know if there was any cavalry within twenty miles of us?'

'Maybe they're too busy getting drunk on the whiskey you sold'em. I'm warning you, you better tell these men to cut us free.'

'Oh, they will cut you, but not free.' Don Alfredo spoke in his precise English, his dark eyes smouldering contemptuously. 'I presume you are the lover man of this bitch?'

'No.' Dawson's grey eyes turned to meet Rose's for moments. 'I am merely doing my duty, carrying out a mission. She is one of ours. We want her back.'

'Is that true?' The old patron flicked the whip tails across Rose's face. 'Wasn't he your — what you say? — fancy man, behind your husband's back?'

'No.' Rose's sage-green eyes blazed defiantly. 'I only wish he had been. I love him, but he does not love me. How

124

can he? You, señor, you disgust me. But I will gladly do anything you wish, anything at all — just let him go. Keep me.'

'Ha! Such a pretty speech. Such romantic notions. You hear that, Ranger? Your woman loves you! Perhaps I should do what she says? She will make an excellent whore. You may have noticed when you so rudely burst in upon us that I, and my maidens, were teaching her the finer points of the erotic arts. But she will not need you alive to perform willingly. This whip will ensure that.'

Anger surged through Dawson, but he struggled futilely against his bonds. A jerk on the noose made him gasp out. Perhaps he could make one last plea. Perhaps this old lecher, with his grand airs, would accept cash for Rose?

'I will pay you for her,' he said. 'You are a businessman. She is up for sale, isn't she?'

'Pay me? What with? My charros found no gold on you.'

'I have been putting some money aside. It was to go towards buying myself some land, some cattle, one of these days. I will pay you a thousand dollars if you let me ride out of here with her.'

Don Alfredo gave him an alert look, greed in his eyes. 'And just how will you do that?'

'I will give you my word of honour. The money will be paid into the bank of Wells Fargo at Santa Fe in New Mexico as soon as we reach safety.'

The old Mexican pursed his lips, considering this, but his face hardened as he felt again at the open cut at the back of his head. 'Maybe I believe you. Maybe you are fool enough to do this. You must be crazy like a love-sick wolf to come riding in here to try to get this one damn woman. Ranger, I admire your bravery. A good try. But nobody — nobody! — touches Don Alfredo de Onate and lives to speak of it.'

He shrieked out the last words as he slashed the whip across Dawson's face.

'I will get a thousand dollars. I will get more than that for her. And I will have my fun with the whore. Just think of that, señor.' He laughed as he slashed the six tails back across Dawson's other cheek. 'Think of what I will be doing to her.'

The Texan tried to jerk his head back to avoid the stinging lashes of the whip, closing his eyes to protect them, gritting his teeth against the pain. 'Do your worst,' he muttered.

'Leave him be!' Rose screamed.

Don Alfredo turned to her, and the lashes whipped across her own cheek, leaving red weals but not drawing blood. He staggered slightly, and stood panting with the exertion. 'Oh, I will leave him be tonight, gringo woman. But tomorrow, when I have rested, you will sit beside me and watch as we hold a fiesta, a farewell to our market before we return to our mountains. You will see how we treat anyone who dares attack Don Alfredo, grandson of a Spanish marquis. You will see him flogged, dragged through the dust to begin with, you will see his skin slowly peeled from his body, the soles sliced from his feet, you will see how, in his desperation, in spite of his horrendous pain, he will try to run away, you will see him maddened and humiliated like a bull, and you will see him slowly die before your eyes. The dogs can gobble his remains, and the Comanches can have his scalp. Comprende?'

'Why?' Rose Cahill stared at him. 'Why are you doing this? I promise I will be good to you. Just let him go.'

'Guard them well.' Don Alfredo raised his arm, and gave a howl of bloodlust revenge. 'Tomorrow is fiesta. Those two spare kegs of whiskey go to the men. Tomorrow we have our fun.'

★ ★ ★

Young Pete Bowen was in the crowd of *vaqueros* and Comanches who watched as Captain Dawson and a young woman were dragged from the big tent and marched over to a nearby covered wagon. There were whoops of excitement as Don Alfredo's foreman shouted out to them about the morrow's festivities.

Pete bit his lip, wondering what to do, as he watched. It looked like it was all over for the cap. Maybe he should do what he said, get his ass out of there before he, too, was sussed out. Somehow, he did not want to leave without a fight.

Across the bonfire, the Mexican, Miguel, saw the youth's face illumined by the rearing tongues of flame. A gold-toothed smile spread across his bearded face and he raised a finger, pointing, 'That's — '

'You what, *amigo?*' one of the *Comancheros* asked, gruffly. 'There gonna be some fun tomorrow, eh?'

'*Si,*' Miguel muttered. 'There gonna be some fun.' He patted the man's shoulder and sidled away around the fire. He reached the youth, pressed his revolver into his back and, a hand on his shoulder, pulled him back into the darkness. 'Señor,' he said. 'It look like your friend in trouble, eh?'

'Yeah,' Pete whispered, huskily. 'It sure does.' He turned to confront his captor. 'And now me, too, eh?'

'Where's that gold I paid your *amigo* for the cattle? Has he got it on him?'

'No. It's hid.'

The firelight gleamed on Miguel's bald head as he poked his sombrero back, and he lightly frisked the youth to make sure he was not carrying it. 'Too bad. I think maybe I have it back before I turn you in.'

'There's a way you could get it back an' welcome to it. You help me git the cap and Miz Cahill away.'

Miguel grinned. 'You crazy. You *gringos*, you all crazy, like you eat the loco weed.'

'Maybe. Maybe not. There's only one way you get that six hundred in gold. You gotta earn it.'

Miguel studied the youth in the

half-darkness with his deep brown, dog-like eyes. 'You come. Get your horses.'

He led Pete, and his mustangs, to a covered *carreta*, a crude wooden wagon with heavy, spoked wheels. Nearby his oxen team grazed. 'My boys are guarding the herd,' he said. '*Mañana* we drive them out. Maybe we go last of all.'

'I get your drift.'

'Where ees the gold?' The broad-chested Miguel rubbed thumb and forefinger together, looking up craftily at the boy who was a head taller than him. 'You geev me now.'

'Nope. My mammy told me nevuh to pay for a meal 'fore I've ate it. Same goes for anythang. You git the gold when I know we're free. You got my word.'

'Your word?' Miguel's voice rose, incredulously. 'You theenk I risk my life, maybe terrible torture, I go against Don Alfredo, on your word?'

'The word of a Texas Ranger,' the

youth shrugged. 'Ain't that good enough?'

Miguel pondered this, tugging at his long moustache points. 'Ees a deal.'

He climbed into the capacious wagon and raised the lid of a keg of gunpowder. 'See? Good stuff, eh?' He lifted it out, grunting as Pete hefted it onto his shoulder. 'Boum! Boum! This make good *fiesta, si?*'

'I get you. You gonna create a diversion. And, under cover of that we go in, get them out.'

'No. You go in.' Miguel cackled with laughter. 'Me create diversion. You get them out, you hide them in wagon. OK?'

'OK,' Pete breathed out sibilantly. 'But hadn't we better wait a while, 'til things quieten down?'

'No, we do eet now. Me *mucho borracho.* Eef I go sleep I no wake up.'

'Yeah?' Pete eyed him quizzically. 'I thought you had whiskey breath. In fact, it near knocked me out. You sure you OK to light this stuff?'

'Yeah, me OK for hour or so. But if I shut eyes — zoom!'

'I hope you ain't gonna wake up, Miguel, and say you remember none of this?'

The *Comanchero* gave another guttural laugh and slapped his shoulder. 'Come. Soon you hear the big bang you act.'

They walked back towards the big tent, stepping silently through the shadows cast by other wagons, listening to the *Comancheros* carousing around the bonfire, the sound of guitars drifting to them. A short distance from the tent, Miguel glanced around, and helped Pete stuff the barrel into a pile of firewood logs. 'Good luck, *gringo*.' He winked, broadly, and walked back into the darkness dropping handfuls of gunpowder in a thin trail behind him.

'Hope he don't blow hisself to smithereens,' Pete said. 'Well, it's now or never, I guess.'

He tipped his Stetson down over

his brow and, his thumbs hitched in his gun-belt, strolled across behind the tent. There was a covered wagon between the tent and the stream, its canvas illumined by a hurricane lamp, which splashed the enlarged shadows of two girls, who were gesticulating their arms, and giggling within. Sitting leaning against a wheel of the wagon on the front end, trussed to it by rope, was a tall man. By the lamp's light Pete could see it was the cap. At the far side rear wheel of the wagon was leaning a young woman in a gleaming satin dress, her shoulders bare. It appeared that she was bound to the wheel, too. Between them were three guards, with carbines in their hands, idly chatting and smoking cigarettes.

The young Texan turned, wandered back, and discreetly secreted himself in the shadows. He slipped out the Smith & Wesson, spun it on a finger, thumbed the hammer, and waited, biting his lip with tension. He determined to kill anyone who got in the way.

'Jeez!' he whistled, as an explosion thundered, belching flame, sending logs hurtling into the night sky. 'That sure went up.'

There were shrill shouts of alarm as men around the bonfire scattered for cover. The reaction of the three guards was to run forward past him, past the big tent, to see what was going on. He had to act fast. He sprinted across the turf, holstering his revolver, pulling out his knife, and slithering down beside Dawson. 'Quick,' he said. 'We gotta hide. I got help.' He slashed at the bonds, and Dawson jumped up, easing his wrists.

There were shouts of confusion coming from the big tent, intensified as another barrel went up. *Kerroum*! Miguel was certainly doing his bit.

Pete slipped across to release Rose Cahill. But his knife scraped on iron. Her wrists were in tight manacles, chained to the iron-rimmed wagon wheel. 'Shee-it!' he groaned, as she glanced sideways at him, her eyes rolling wildly.

'What's going on?' Dawson asked. 'Are you all right, Rose?'

'She's in irons. There's no way we gonna git her loose.'

'Hell.' Dawson stared at her, and touched her cheek with his fingers. He glanced back and saw shadows of men returning around the big tent. 'If we had a file.'

'Come on, Cap. We've got no time.'

'Chas, go,' Rose cried. 'Save yourself. Forget me.'

'No way,' Dawson said, rising from his knees, his fingers outstretched. 'I'm not giving you up to him.'

'Come on.' Pete caught hold of his jacket and dragged him away as the guards shouted out, and raised their carbines. They fired, bullets bouncing off the wagon, too close for comfort, spurting the dust about their legs as they backed away. 'They asked for it,' the youth said, his revolver in his fist, cocking and firing fast — one, two, three — the guards spun and tumbled into the dust. 'I sure had a bellyful of these boys.'

They turned and ran, darting away back among the wagons and camp-fires, Pete leading the way, slowing down, acting casual, making sure they were not observed by their pursuers as he reached Miguel's wagon.

'Git in here, Cap. You'll be safe with Miguel. He'll be back soon.' He went to his mustang, produced the pouch of golden eagles from the saddle-bag. 'Here, I've promised him these.'

'Where you going?' Dawson looked distraught as he caught the pouch, and watched the youth swing into the saddle. 'What you doing?'

'I'm gonna play rabbit,' he grinned. 'See if they can catch me.'

'Don't be a fool. You haven't got a chance,' Dawson hissed at him. 'Not against these riders, against Comanches. They'll track you down. Hide in here with me. Ranger, that's an order.'

'I allus bin a bit hard of hearin', Cap. Didn' I tell ya?' Pete whirled the mustang around. 'See ya later. I'll be watchin' and waitin'.'

Dawson watched the youth spur the horse, go streaking away, leaping over corral thorn hedges, weaving through camp-fires, the mustang's hooves pounding, his tail and mane flailing, as men shouted and ran out, and shots were fired. And then there were shrill howls of Comanches, and still the mustang's hooves kept pounding, the rider hung low over his neck, splashing along the stream, a dark, slight figure, turning to glance back, to judge the distance of his pursuers, as men jumped onto broncos and headed after him.

'He's made it.' Dawson breathed out with relief, standing on the tailboard of the wagon, seeing the moon gleam on the river, on the shod hooves of the mustang as he hightailed it out of the Cañon de Las Lagrimas. But for how long? 'Hang on in there, Pete. They ain't got us yet.'

'Howdy, *señor*,' a voice said, as a rifle poked him in the back. 'Is that gold you got in your hand? You just hand it to me.' Miguel gave a roar of laughter. 'I wonder how much Don Alfredo will reward me for catching you?'

8

He galloped out of the Cañon de Las
Lagrimas whipping the mustang from
side to side with an end of his lariat, the
speed of his movement splaying back
the brim of his black Stetson, hung low
over the horse's neck, the coarse mane
flaying his face, peering across the dark
plain streaked silver and black by the
big globe of moon. The tough buffalo
grass was cut by the iron-rimmed
wheels of the heavy *carretas* and the
hooves of their horses as, loaded with
trade booty, they had headed towards
the meeting place of the tribes. He
figured it best to follow this trail, both
because it would be safer for his horse
to go along without stumbling, and his
own trail would be lost in the quagmire
of prints. It was a feisty, deep-chested
mustang and it ate up the ground, its
hooves sounding out a staccato rhythm

beneath them. Pete heard an ululating howl behind him and knew that the Comanches and *Comancheros* had taken up the chase. The trail headed towards a spur of rocks up ahead. If he could reach that in good time he might outride them. He did not think much of his chances if he did not.

But, at his age, death did not bother him. He could not imagine what his own would be like. He did not deem it possible. All he knew was a wild youthful excitement, the surging of his blood, the thrill of being chased, the joy of being alive. On he galloped, letting the mustang pick its own course, rejoining the meandering stream, leaping and splashing across it, and on into the night. He swerved around the dark outcrop of rocks and began to look ahead for a hiding place. Just the spot! Halfway up the dust slope was a bizarrely shaped array of wind-eroded columns, the valley winding on round another bend not far off. He dragged on a rein and ploughed the mustang up to them, tumbling from the saddle and dragging the horse into the shadows. Just in time! There was a thunder of hooves as the pursuers came charging around the spur, a blood-thirsty screaming of naked, feathered Comanches as they led the chase, the *vaqueros* eating their dust. In the darkness they did not notice his trail departing from all the other tracks. He watched them race on past, and grinned as he saw them go thudding along towards the next bend of the river.

He would do what Terrazos did, try to wipe out his trail. He took his blanket and ran down, and began swiftly flapping at the dust of the steep climb making his way back up to *las columnas*. It was not perfect, but an improvement on clear hoof-prints. Out of breath, he reached the safety of the rocks only to find the mustang dropping a steaming heap of manure. 'Aw, that's a dead give-away if they come up here. Trust a damn bronc to leave a calling card.'

He looked up at the rocks. There was a fault line running diagonally up the cliff. With a little luck he might get the horse up there. If not, or if they came back and spotted him, he would have to make a stand, fight them off until his ammunition was spent. It was a hairy climb in the darkness, up the precipitous cliff, dragging the reluctant, wild-eyed mustang. But they made it to the rim. Again, not a second too soon. Pete hung onto the reins and peered over the edge as the posse of Indians and New Mexicans came cantering back, looking up as they did so at the jagged cliffs. Pete ducked down, swung into the saddle, and headed off. He planned to keep to the high ground. The moon was rising high, illuminating the hazardous, trackless waste before him. By daylight he hoped to have put a good many miles between himself and any pursuers.

★ ★ ★

'If you're planning to hand me over to Don Alfredo he might not be well pleased to hear that you arranged that little gunpowder plot.' Chas Dawson smiled grimly at the chubby, moustached Miguel, who had him covered with his rifle. 'Not that I'd want to snitch on you.'

'Don Alfredo has offered five hundred dollars for the Ranger's head' — Dawson, too, had heard the *vaqueros* calling this out before they rode out — 'or that of his accomplice.'

'You're my accomplice now.'

Miguel stroked his sun-blackened dome and considered this before spitting out a brown squirt of baccy juice. 'Severed heads don't talk. All it takes is a couple of machete blows.'

'You wouldn't do that, Miguel. You're not that kind of guy.'

'You theenk so?'

'I offered Don Alfredo a thousand if he let the Texan girl go free. The money's yours if you help me get her back.'

'Fool! You got no thousand dollars. You lie.'

'I got it. All I got to do is write a promissory note to you and sign it and you can collect it from the Wells Fargo bank, Santa Fe, or Las Vegas, or wherever you choose. It's the modern way of doing business. Ain't you heard? Saves lugging all them heavy bags of gold coin about.'

'Gold iss good.' Miguel groomed his long moustachios, thoughtfully.

'You pick up your gold in New Mexico. I've told you.'

'How I trust you? You a *gringo*.'

'You'll just have to.' Dawson hopefully extended a hand. 'Shake on it?'

'How we get this *señora* free? She under close guard.'

'We'll think of something as we go along. The element of surprise works wonders.'

Miguel stared at him with muddy eyes, put up his rifle and gripped his hand. 'It a deal. That Don Alfredo, pah! He allus cheat me. He one no-good big shot.'

'Where will he take her?'

'Don Alfredo has fortress across
border New Mexico at Los Portales, El
Rancho del Oro. Maybe he sell her to
rich rancher. Or maybe to the *bandido*,
El Borracho. He has hide-out in
mountains. He a real bad man. Even
Apache scared of him.'

'How far's the Rancho del Oro from
here?'

'Maybe a hundred miles, mostly over
desert.'

'And how much further's this El
Borracho's hideout?'

'Anudder hundred and fifty miles or
so. Across the Pecos valley, along the
Rio Hondo, an' up the Rio Bonito. He
has stronghold up under El Capitan
mountain. Nobody can get in there.'

'Yeah? Well, I come near on five
hundred miles already up the Brazos
and I ain't giving up now.'

'Thass wha' I hear. You Texas Ranger,
you never give up 'til you get your
man.' Miguel gave a roar of laughter.

146

'Or your woman.'

'Or my woman.' It felt strange to Dawson saying that, knowing that he still felt the same about her, in spite of that nauseating thing she had been . . . she must have been forced into it. Hadn't she been the wife of Jake Cahill, that fat bully? That must have been pretty unbearable for her, too.

'You're right. Only thing that stops us is a bullet in the heart. Once set on a mission the Rangers don't give up.'

'*Gringo.*' Miguel leaned forward and slapped his shoulder. 'I like you. I gonna trust you for that gold. Maybe we get her back, but I sure don' know how.'

'I jest feel so damn sorry for the poor kid, what she's been through, what she's still got to go through. It sickens me.'

'Stranger, thass why they call this the Canyon of Tears.'

★ ★ ★

147

Pete kept the mustang moving across the harsh terrain until high noon. He was glad of the leather chaps to protect his legs from the sharp rocks and thorns. It was hard work finding his way through the boulders and scrub, occasionally striking a path trod by a herd of wild goats or sheep. He tried to keep near the rim of the valley but not in sight. He was glad to find a shallow sandstone cave in a tangle of thicket which gave shade. He needed to rest the horse. The lack of water was his main problem. He had sucked on a pebble to try to assuage his own thirst, but the mustang had been sweating hard and needed a good drink. The youth poured a drop from his wooden canteen into a shallow hole for the beast to lap up, and allowed himself a taste. There was river-water down the valley. Maybe in the night they would slip down there. He had thrown a stick at a jack-rabbit and killed it. He skinned this and decided it would be safe to light a small fire to cook it. He had been riding since dawn and had seen no sign of life on this high plateau. It was just a windswept wilderness. He reckoned they had given up the chase.

When he had eaten his fill, he lounged in the shade of the ledge of cave and gazed out across the scrub. It was strange to be alone, many hundreds of miles from the safety of his own home, in the middle of this vast hostile country, with only one friend, and not sure whether he was still alive. He hoped so. Miguel had seemed an honest sort. There were good and bad on both sides. Pete did not feel lonesome or afraid. He loved being out in the wide open unknown spaces, under the great saucer of sky. He liked the sense of danger, of living on the edge. It made him feel alive, that every moment counted. He was even pleased, in a way, that he had killed or wounded those three men with three fast shots, fired from the hip, automatically, or instinctively, fanning the hammer down with the heel of his left hand. He had never wanted to kill, but it had been them or him, simple as that. And it proved he had mastered the revolver. What was it the cap had called him — a natural? Not a natural-born killer, a natural gunman. He felt proud that he had proved he could protect himself, and the cap, too.

'Jeez!' he whistled. 'If they could see me now back at Catfish Falls. A Ranger, with six badmen already accounted for.'

Or was it seven? He was already beginning to lose count. He lay and daydreamed about that other life, his boyhood life, the arduous life on the small farm, up before dawn to feed the hogs, hewing logs, ploughing the earth. It was not the hard work, the drudgery, he objected to; it was the constant repetition, the same thing, the same faces, day after day. He had needed to escape, to go see this wild country.

Pete came to his senses with a jerk as two Comanches appeared as if from nowhere before him, one with a lance gripped hard and pointed at him, the other with an arrow in his bow drawn tight. And a third Comanche suddenly appeared, dropping down from the ledge of the cave, landing lightly on the balls of his moccasined feet. They wore little more than loin cloths, their sun-bronzed bodies wiry and muscular, their eyes questing, but darkly cold.

The third one had a flintlock musket, hung with scalps, pointed at Pete. His head had been shaved bald, except for a top-knot roach of hair into which two hawk's feathers had been threaded. His eyes in their harsh slits were like black pebbles. He appeared to be the leader for he shouted out angrily, words of an incomprehensible language. It sounded like 'Kwah she-ho.' He indicated Pete should get to his feet.

The Texan youth did so, slowly, holding his hands away from his hips, his right-hand fingers fluttering over the Smith & Wesson. Should he try to take them? Or would that be suicidal — he did not relish a lance, arrow and ball in him, simultaneously? 'OK fellas,' he said. 'You got the drop on me. Maybe it was a mistake to make that fire.'

The shaven-headed Comanche kept his finger of his right hand on the trigger of the long musket, and pointed with his left at the S & W in its holster, flicking his finger for Pete to give it him.

'No way,' the young Texan drawled. 'You wan' it, you gotta earn it.' He fixed them with his dark eyes, nodding calmly and slowly drew out his hunting knife, a six-inch blade of best Solingen steel. He pointed it at the Indian and made sign with his free hand. 'You — me. We fight for it.'

The Comanche looked puzzled at first, and then chuckled, shaking his head. 'Firestick,' he shouted. 'You give.'

'So you know some English? You know what *no* means?'

The two braves behind the shaven-headed one had twigged what Pete suggested and, grinning, levelled a volley of words at the musket-man's back. 'What they sayin'? You a yeller-bellied creep won't accept the challenge of some white kid?'

'Hach!' The Comanche warrior screamed like a hawk seizing its prey and placed the musket aside. He, too, drew his hunting knife as the other two fell back, still with their weapons poised, and watched, their eyes alert.

The Comanche crouched, his razor-sharp knife ready, and for moments he and the youth faced each other, moving around, each waiting for the other to make first move. Suddenly the Indian sprang in, and slashed. Pete pulled in his stomach, felt his shirt rip, a tingling across his abdomen. The Comanche had drawn first blood. They circled around each other again, the Indian's movements, the muscled thighs and arms freer, unrestrained by clothes. Pete, for his part, shuffled in his heavy spurred boots. Again the Comanche leapt in and the boy was lucky he had the natural reflexes to jerk back his head or it would have been his throat cut.

He swallowed his fear and at the same time a surge of fury made him go on the attack, slashing like a swordsman with the knife. The Comanche dodged from side to side avoiding his blade, his eyes fixed on him. Then he hurled himself at the Texan, his knife aimed at his chest. Pete tried to step back, but slipped on the smooth rock. As he went down he stuck up a boot and sent the Indian somersaulting over him. The youth followed the roll and landed on top of the Comanche, taller than him, holding him down, pinning him with his knees and boots, twisting his knife wrist away, and pricking his own blade to his throat. 'You had enough?' he gasped.

The Comanche stared back at him defiantly. Pete was about to let him up, but the other two were yelling at him, excitedly. The one with the lance knelt beside him, stabbing it up and down. What were they saying? That he had won, that he had to *kill* him? Well, he was not playing in the schoolyard now. If that was the way they wanted it? He plunged the knife deep into the jugular. A fountain of blood spouted over him, and the Indian's eyes glazed over.

'Yuk!' The boy stared at the corpse for seconds, the now lifeless bronze mask, with a kind of horror.

He climbed slowly to his feet and faced the other two warriors. 'Now I guess I gotta take on you two.' He beckoned them to him with a cupped hand, the hunting knife ready, dripping blood. 'Who's gonna be first?'

The two Comanches stared at him, haughty and impassive. One let out a shrill yelp, and they turned on their heels and disappeared as swiftly as they had arrived, and as silently. Pete left the mouth of the cave and saw them jogging away on their ponies through the scrub, their long hair flayed by the whining wind.

He returned and looked at the dead Comanche. 'Waal,' he drawled, 'he had two chances, same as me. He died a warrior's death. Better than waitin' to git old, I guess.'

His mustang was daintily nibbling at the thorns finding sustenance, unconcerned. What had it to do with him what fool men did? Pete swung onto his back. 'Come on, hoss. Let's git.'

9

All thoughts of *fiesta* were forgotten by Don Alfredo. He ranted at his men as useless lazy bastards for being unable to catch the Ranger. He promised the two barrels of whiskey to three warriors, renown as the Comanches' best trackers, if they brought him in. They returned empty-handed, or two of them did, shrugged mutely when asked if they had seen any sign of the *Yanqui*. He presumed the third had taken it in mind to wander off across the prairie, as Indians were prone to. Indeed, now the bartering was done, the tribes were packing up their scant belongings, and drifting away to disappear among the scarred ravines and sparse grasslands of the Staked Plains. By-passed by frontier development, for a few more years it would remain their own domain.

Don Alfredo decided to punish his

men by keeping the whiskey for his own consumption. The lump on the back of his head still throbbed from the Ranger's revolver blow and he vowed in lurid detail what he would do when he caught him, hang him up by his heels over his fire to begin with, not realizing that he was resting in a covered *carreta* not 100 yards away.

'I should have shot him when I had him,' he said.

He had much to do, and gave orders to move out his column of 2,000 stolen Texan cattle, and 400 broncos and mules. He was a tad worried that there might be other Rangers around because it was obvious Dawson must have had accomplices — three dead men pointed to that. He made sure Rose Cahill did not escape by chaining her to the wagon wheel at night, and cuffing her in irons in the covered wagon when they were on the move. She was a valuable property.

Miguel watched the caravan of Don Alfredo's carts, horses and cattle go wambling away through the mud. A sudden summer downpour had turned the trail into a quagmire. The Mexican slave-dealers and horse-traders had packed up and headed south with their booty towards the border, or maybe the Horsehead Pass into southern New Mexico. He, himself, would drive his herd of cows and horses in the wake of Don Alfredo along the little-known trail into the hills across the border of the eastern section of the state that had only in recent years been surrendered into Union hands. *El Presidente*, General Santa Anna, had disgracefully abandoned them to live under the rule of the *Yanqui*. But Miguel was a pragmatist, and guessed he had to make the best of the new order of things. Some of the *gringos* were not so bad. He wondered if he could trust Ranger Dawson's word as he cracked his whip across the backs of the oxen pulling their wagon. Yes, he knew he was an honest man, if deluded by passion for his captured woman. It would do no harm to have a Ranger as a friend.

And, from his eyrie on the cliffside of the valley, the young Texan watched the mile-long line of cattle, horses and wagons go plodding on their way and wondered when Captain Dawson would choose to make his break. The rainwater, caught in pools in the rocks, had come as a blessing. But he figured it would be safe enough to descend to the easier route of the valley if he kept a discreet distance behind. The *vaqueros* were hardly likely to come back looking for him now.

★ ★ ★

In spite of her chafed wrists from being constantly manacled, Rose Cahill was in reasonably good health and spirits. The girls fed her and looked after her, putting ointment on her wrists, and chattering mischievously. After the first day's journey when they reached a stretch of water called Buffalo Lake, she was allowed to bathe with them. At times she was cheerful that Ranger Dawson had escaped; she hoped against hope that she might see him again; and then her spirits sloughed, for what could he do against fifty or so armed *Comancheros*? Maybe it would be best if he gave up this foolish idea of rescuing her? What did he want her for, anyway? She was tainted fruit now.

At least, for the time being, Don Alfredo had lost interest in his promised plan of training her in the erotic arts, as the disgusting lecher described his attentions. He was in the saddle all day riding back and forth, chivvying his men and the herd along, and by the time they had made camp was far too exhausted to indulge in such things. After supper, when the girls joined him in his tent, he generally fell fast asleep. He was an old greyhair, after all. Sometimes Rose thought that if she were forced to be his wife or mistress it would not be such a terrible fate. In his aristocratic, haughty way, he was quite amusing and kindly. Apart from striking her across the face that once, he had not whipped or beaten her, or played games of mental torture like Joaquin Terrazos. Where she wondered was he? She had an uneasy feeling they might meet again. But what did fill her with dread was the thought of the man Don Alfredo planned to sell her to *El Borracho*, The Drunkard, the girls called him. They had met him on his occasional visit to Don Alfredo's *hacienda*. A butcher, a torturer of men and animals, a sadistic brute, of whose drunken fury men went in fear. 'Ach!' Celeste had rolled her eyes. 'I pity you. He is not a good one.'

★   ★   ★

The lake was well named for a vast herd of buffalo were wallowing and watering in its shallows, only lumbering on their way when the *vaqueros* shot a few for meat. After a few miles they slowed their pace and began to graze again, dotting the scant grassland with their brown shapes as far as the eye could see.

Young Pete Bowen reached the lake the morning after the caravanserai of *Comacheros* had moved on its way following the Tierra Blanca Creek. He was not familiar with bison and they were between him and the water where he wished to fill his canteen and give his horse a drink. He made a yipping cry and edged his horse through them and they hardly bothered to move out of his way. Suddenly, however, a big hunchbacked bull took exception to his presence. He glowered through his short-sighted eyes, lowered his stubby but viciously pronged horns, gave an angry bellow, pawed the earth, and charged. When he saw him coming Pete tried to whirl his horse out of the way, but the mustang screamed as the horns tore into his side, and the vast weight of the bull bowled them over. The next thing he knew he was on the ground, a leg trapped beneath the mustang which was giving death kicks as the bull tore out his entrails. When the horse finally ceased its terrified clamour of agony, his head dropping back, teeth snarlingly exposed, Pete met the buff's dark and stony eyes, and wondered what to do. He could not reach for his musket and his revolver was somehow trapped beneath him. The bull continued to paw and gore the horse, and then it moved around it to the youth. Pete gritted his teeth and winced at the prospect of those sharp little horns gouging into him. He dimly remembered hearing that the best thing to do was to lie still. Well, he could not run away. He closed his eyes as the buffalo's harsh-breathing face came closer, examining him. As if for an age he waited for attack. But the only attack that came was a huge foul-smelling tongue that began licking his face. What the hell? he thought, as the rasping tongue kept on licking, and licking . . . and licking. He began to think he planned to lick him to death. Why the beast chose to lick at him like that he did not know, but, at least, it was better than being gored. It seemed like a full half-hour the buff' kept licking at him, and by the time he lost interest and trotted back to his females, the youth's cheek was red raw.

'Whoowee!' With a lot of heaving he managed to get his leg free, but had to leave one spurred boot and one leather chap beneath the mustang. He hopped around in his stockinged foot, trying to bring back circulation. The only good thing was that the leg was not broken. The musket was beneath the horse, but he still had his revolver. He looked around at the bare prairie covered with brown slowly drifting herds. Not a human in sight. The *Comancheros* had gone on their way. 'How the hail am I supposed to catch 'em up?' he wailed.

* * *

A shimmering plain of waterless desert had to be crossed before the great herd reached the *hacienda* of Don Alfredo. Perhaps this was the reason why Anglo cattlemen had, as yet, shown little interest in the grasslands of New Mexico. This, plus the natural barrier of the Staked Plains ruled by Comanches and *Comancheros*. The southern route was even more hazardous for herding cattle, three days without water via the dreaded Horsehead Crossing and no white cattle drover had attempted it. The main access to New Mexico was from the north along the Santa Fe trail. Thus most of this vast territory of Apache-infested mountains, cleft by river valleys, was sparsely populated by settlers, and most of those *Latinos*. The US Army maintained a presence at Fort Sumner and Fort Stanton but their interest was in pacifying Navajo and Mescalero warriors. Elsewhere, men such as Don Alfredo were left to enforce their own law like feudal lords. Long custom told him he could get the cattle through the desert without too many dropping by the wayside and he had his *Comancheros* press them at a whip-cracking hard pace by day and night.

When Rose saw the fortified adobe walls of the Rancho del Oro flushed cherry red by the rays of a titanic sunset she knew why it was named the Golden Ranch. The vast mass of horn-tossing hides, the parched herd, went at a run when they smelt the water tanks, those behind pushing the leaders on past, so the *vaqueros* had their work cut out settling them down. When they had put on some fat Don Alfredo would sell them on, either as beef for the soldiers and the Indians on the reservations, or to other ranchers scattered about the state.

'Welcome to my house,' he said to Rose, unlocking her wrist manacles, and handing her down from the covered *carreta*. 'Tonight we will celebrate. I have special plans for you.'

★   ★   ★

A few miles away, in the dusty, run-down little town of Los Portales,

Joaquin Terrazos was already celebrating. He sprawled in the town's *cantina*, a bottle of *aguadiente* gripped in one fist, his other fondling the breast of a dark-eyed *poblana* reclined on his knee. He jogged her body frenziedly in time with the crashing and stamping of a fandango, as her sister *chollas* clicked their fingers, rattled their high heels, and whirled their satin skirts to reveal their dark, sinuous legs.

'They're an ugly, cross-eyed bunch, ain't they?' Terrazos roared, as he nearly shook his poor girl's teeth from her head. 'But they sure know how to dance.'

The fat and sweating leader of the combo parped at his battered trumpet and sent forth a set of ear-piercing notes, as his 'musicians' on drums, flute and guitar, racketed along to his lead. He ducked with fright as Terrazos pulled out a fearful-looking weapon and crashed out two shots over his head into the roof. But still he played on. If the bandit Terrazos was in the mood to celebrate it did not do to argue with him.

The weapon brandished by Terrazos was a curious one. Its grip was walnut, its magazine brass, and its steel barrel a good twelve inches. They called it the Volcanic .41, a lever action repeating carbine. It was like an over-sized revolver and came with a separate cleaning rod, and a detachable steel butt stock for long-range use. It amused Terrazos to use it as a revolver, and it was certainly lighter, and more easily concealed, than a regular carbine.

'*Vamos!*' He tipped the girl off his knee and she bumped to the floor. She was as dark-skinned as an Apache, and probably had their blood in her. She looked up at him, startled, and extended her palm, beseechingly. He flipped her a silver dollar. He could afford to be generous. He had plenty. And he had a plan to make plenty more. He had already taken his pleasure with her, and with the other whores in the three days he had been running riot in the town. 'Silence,' he shouted, crashing out another shot, and smashing a bottle behind the bar. 'This racket is making my head spin.'

The dancers whirled to a halt as the music faded, while the owner of the *cantina*, dressed like most of the others in white cotton pyjamas and straw hat, watched to see what this maniac, Terrazos, would get up to next. But the bandit was getting bored. He lurched over to a group of men, dressed in the leathers of *vaqueros*, and hung with iron, who were playing cards in a corner.

'Deal me in,' he snarled, slumping down beside them.

★   ★   ★

The interior of the Rancho del Oro *hacienda* was cool and shady, sparsely furnished, but its flagstone floors and kitchens kept spotlessly clean by Don Alfredo's daughters and serving women. Rose was shown to a bedroom where there was a huge four-poster bed of carved oak. Juana laughed harshly, as she bathed, primped, painted, perfumed, and dressed the white girl in low-cut satin of emerald hue. 'The master plans to romp with you tonight.'

'Oh, no,' Rose groaned, and looked around, once more, for some way of escape. The narrow window looked out onto a courtyard. It was open to the night air but barred. And even if she reached the stables, stole a horse, how could she get past the armed guards who patrolled the high walls and wooden gate around the house? And, if she did get out of this prison, how find her way back through that desert, or north-west through this bleak, rugged land to Fort Sumner? Hope, as they say, springs eternal, and there still glimmered inside her a faint hope of rescue by Charles Dawson, or even, perhaps, by a platoon of US Cavalry. But that would be a miracle. Impossible. Futile to even dream of it. She could fight, scratch, spit, kick, beg the old *hidalgo* not to further dishonour her, but what would be the use of that? He had the power to do with her whatever he wished. As she brushed, lethargically, at her luxuriant hair, a sense of impotence overcame her, and she prepared to meet her distasteful fate.

'Why so sullen, my sweet one?' Rose flinched as Don Alfredo leaned to pinch at her cheek as she sat beside him at dinner. 'Those rosy lips were meant for smiling. Isn't the food to your liking?'

Rose had hardly touched the soup, the tortillas and salad and beef steak, and now contemplated, moodily, the large ripe peach set before her. 'I have no appetite for the food, or for you,' she murmured. 'Why can't you just sell me back to my people? Ranger Dawson has said he will pay you. I know he is a man of his word.'

'Enough, girl. I've heard all this before. Are you looking for a good whipping? I'd love to see my 'cat' cut red weals across your white buttocks.

And it surely will if you don't change your tune. I assure you the only thing Ranger Dawson will receive from me is a bullet in his guts if we ever meet again. So, cheer yourself.'

Don Alfredo was sitting at the head of a long banqueting table. Across from Rose was his eldest son, Jaime, a man of middling years, his dark hair flecked with silver, who had been borne in by two men for his legs were paralysed. Apparently, his spine had been crushed when his horse fell on him, and he was numb from the waist down.

'I have a damn good mind to marry you, myself,' Don Alfredo growled, patting her thigh beneath the table and making her visibly jump. 'I need a male heir. Jaime here, as you see, is useless. And my other son, Francisco, went off to make his fortune in the California gold fields and I have not heard from him since. All my spoiled bitches of daughters have produced are granddaughters. Of course, I have fathered plenty of bastards. But I need a legal heir to carry on my line. A fine white girl like you would be ideal. What do you say? You would be rich, respected everywhere you go.'

'I . . . I cannot have children,' Rose lied. 'The doctors have told me so.'

'Pah! What do doctors know? What you need is a good stud bull like me.' He laughed, gutturally, and squeezed her knee again. 'There may be snow on top of the mountain, but there's a volcano down below. Tonight' — he flickered a wink at her — 'we will continue your education. Aren't you looking forward to that?'

'No.' She met Jaime's dark, suffering eyes. 'Can't you help me? Can't you tell him that it is against the law to hold me here like this, that he could be severely punished?'

'Forgive me, *señorita*.' Jaime shook his head, sadly. 'What can I do? What my father says is law. I certainly congratulate him on his taste.'

'Yeah, not bad, eh?' Don Alfredo patted his son's shoulder. 'It's a pity you could not — '

Rose saw Jaime flinch at this remark. He was as much a prisoner of the old man as she. She began to cut a knife into the peach. 'Perhaps I will marry you,' she sighed. 'It would be better than being sold to this *El Borracho*.'

'It certainly would.' Don Alfredo touched her hand with delight. 'At last you are beginning to see sense. Don't worry, I will be good to you. Whatever you want will be yours.'

'Except freedom,' Rose whispered.

10

The young Texan walked on across the desert. It was night-time but the three-quarter moon had yet to wane and its light threw a ghostly glow over the scene. He had no difficulty following the trail, the sand churned up by thousands of cattle, wagons and horses, going on straight as an arrow across the seemingly endless waste. His main difficulty was walking in a straight line. His long legs had begun to give way under him and he lurched, at times, like a drunk. His wooden canteen of water had been crushed under the ton weight of the fallen horse. Maybe its bulk had saved his leg? Whatever, since leaving the river not a drop of water had touched his lips. His shirt was coldly damp with perspiration. Where, he wondered, did all the sweat come from? He had trudged on and on, his bare foot cut and bloody, the uncomfortable high-heeled boot blistering his other heel. He knew the body had to be constantly water-cooled or it would fail. When he reached the desert his spirit quailed. How far could he go? He knew a man was regarded as doomed if he was without a horse or water in this sort of country. He limped on throughout the day, on across the burning sands, his tongue swollen, his lips parched. With nightfall he kept going. At least, in darkness he did not have the shimmering mirages of water to lure him off course. He had thought at one point he was approaching a blue lake and had broken into a run until he realized it was just an illusion. On and on the desert stretched. He had begun to stagger and fall. But he climbed back to his feet. He did not dare rest for fear he might not get up again.

Suddenly he saw a horseman riding towards him, coming at a fast lope, ploughing through the dunes. Pete froze, thinking it might be an Indian.

No, he could see no lance, no feathers. The rider was wearing a tall sombrero. Maybe it was a *Comanchero* sent to see if anyone was following. He looked for cover, but there was no place to hide. He knelt down and drew his Smith & Wesson, aiming it across his wrist, unsteadily. If the rider had a rifle and was looking for trouble he had no chance.

Closer and closer the horseman came, as the youth cocked the small calibre revolver and prepared to fight. Suddenly the rider raised his hand in greeting. 'Cap?' the youth gasped out. 'Cap? Is that you?'

It was, indeed, Captain Dawson, in his Mexican outfit, reining in, jumping from the saddle, supporting the youth. 'I come to look for you. I was wondering where the hell you'd got to.' He took his canteen of water, uncorked it and held it to Pete's mouth. 'Whoa, boy. Just take a few drops. Not too much. Come on. Can you climb up behind me? Let's go.' He turned the big-chested mustang and headed back the way he had come. 'We'll be clear of this desert by dawn and in the hills.'

'Wha' you gonna do?' Pete mumbled, hanging on to the cantle. 'You still on her tail, Cap?'

'Yes. But, each night they stopped, that old Mexican had his wagons drawn up in a defensive circle, his tent in the centre of them, his guards prowling around. There was no way of getting close. Now they've reached his ranch house, armed men manning the high walls.'

When they rested at dawn to brew up black coffee and Cap Dawson passed a tin mug of it across, Pete murmured through his blistered lips, 'Don't it sometimes seem we're on a wild goose chase, that we ain't never gonna catch up with that gal?'

Dawson frowned, and stared at their fire. 'Don't say that, Pete. You're talking 'bout the woman I love. You're free to go. But I ain't never gonna give up the search.'

Pete studied the Ranger, puzzled. What was it with grown men? There were plenty of women in the world. How come they could get so obsessed and upset by one girl? What was this crazy thing called love? Here it was smiting a strong man like the cap, who was used to riding free. 'I sure hope I nevuh git bit by that bug.'

'What's that?'

'Nuthin',' the boy grinned. 'Less go git her.'

'Yes, but to do that we need a plan. And we probably need reinforcements. I think I should ride to Fort Sumner.'

'They weren't int'rested in helping you at Fort Worth.'

'Yes, I know . . . but we've got to try. We've got to, Pete.'

*   *   *

Joaquin Terrazos was losing badly in the poker game. In fact, he had been spending so wildly since hitting town most of the $500 from Don Alfredo had

180

burned a hole in his pocket. He looked across, meanly, at the *hombre* who was so slick at the game of bluff, who was reaching out hands to pull in his winnings of gold coin. Terrazos scratched nervously at the white scar on his cheek with his left-hand fingers, his eyes narrowed, as he hissed, 'You got that by damned cheating.' His right hand brought out the Volcanic from under his coat and he blasted the *hombre* in the chest as he tried to scramble to his feet. The man went tumbling backwards, hit the wall and slowly slid down, leaving a bloody streak from his bullet-exited back. His sombrero slipped from his head as he lolled forward. Terrazos blew down the barrel of the Volcanic. 'You saw him. He try to draw on me. Nobody cheat Joaquin Terrazos.' He leaned forward greedily, and scooped the jackpot, filling his pockets. 'Hey, what you guys look at? You got argument?'

The other mean-faced men, as scurvy

181

a bunch of frontier scum as any who drifted through Los Portales, shrugged indifferently. It was no big deal. And Terrazos was buying them drinks, shouting to the musicians to start playing again.

'You boys ready to make some real money?'

'Where at?'

'At the Rancho del Oro.'

'What we gonna do, rustle some cows?'

'No. I got unfinished business with Don Alfredo.'

Terrazos lowered his voice as he outlined the kind of business he had in mind. He flicked gold coins across to each of the seven *hombres*. They nodded, got to their feet, gave the whores hugs and kisses, followed him out, and climbed on their mustangs. They went at a fast jog out of town, through the strangely shaped columns of rock which gave the town its name. Out they rode through the moonlight towards the grey folded mountains.

Don Alfredo lit a cheroot from a burning candle and smiled, foxily, at Rose Cahill, glancing at the enticing cleft of her bosom. 'It is getting late,' he said, breathing out smoke, and raising a glass of brandy. 'I think it is time for your lesson. I have been waiting a long time for this.'

There was a rap on the door and a *vaquero*, a rifle slung over his shoulder, entered. 'Joaquin Terrazos is outside, *señor*. He wants to speak to you.'

'What does he want at this time of night?'

'He would not say, *patron*. Only that it is very important. Something to do with that Ranger who has been following you.'

'The Ranger?' The old man tossed his white mane, angrily. 'Has he killed him?'

'I don't know. He is with seven other men. Perhaps they have news of him.'

'Keep them in the courtyard. Send

him in on his own.' When the *Comanchero* had gone Don Alfredo saw Rose's alarmed face. 'What's the matter? Are you afraid I might sell you back to Terrazos? Don't worry. He probably has some cock and bull story to wheedle more money out of me. I will inform him I don't need his services, that you are to be my bride.'

Before Rose could reply, the guard burst in leading Terrazos, who had two armed *Comancheros* following him.

'Don Alfredo, forgive the intrusion.' Terrazos doffed his hat with exaggerated courtesy and smiled at him. 'I have important information. Those two Texan spies. They have been seen.'

'Seen? What do you mean.'

'Seen. A *peon* told me. They were riding two-up along the trail, then one set off on his own towards Fort Sumner.'

'Fort Sumner?' The old man, in his pearl-decorated suit, his lace shirt and scarlet bandanna, rose to his feet, alarmed. 'Why should he go there?'

'Why do you think? To raise the cavalry. To attack you. To rescue' — he pointed a finger at Rose — 'her!'

'They will be too late. By the time they get here I will have married her. Here, in my private chapel. My own chaplain will perform the ceremony this night. The young lady knows what is best for her. She has consented to be my bride.'

'Don Alfredo. You think she will consent now she knows the troopers will come looking for her? Of course, she won't. Or, if she does, she will say you forced her. I have a better idea. Sell her back to me for five hundred dollars and I will take her to *El Borracho*.'

'No.' Rose spoke in a low voice. 'Don't give me to him. I will marry you tonight, I promise.'

'You see.' Don Alfredo opened his palms, and resumed his seat. 'She does not want to leave me. When they arrive we will be legally wed. Anyway, if I wish to I can hide her. They will never find her. Or, should I want to sell her, my own men can take her to *El Borracho*. So, I have no need for your services, my friend. Thank you for being so kind as to bring me this information. For that I will pay a hundred dollars. Thank you, Joaquin. Have a glass of bourbon before you go.'

'I see, it's like that, is it?' Terrazos smiled, his lips curling back over his teeth, more like a snarl. 'OK. One hundred will help me out. I am glad to have been of service to you, *patron*. Let me just tell my men that they will not be needed. They had hoped to profit from the girl.' He strolled over to the barred window and called down to his *hombres* in the courtyard. 'It is off. You can go back to town. Don Alfredo thanks us for our offer, but is not interested.'

Terrazos walked back to the head of the table, and as the old man filled his glass with bourbon, he grinned, wolfishly, over at Rose. 'To the happiness of the loving couple.' He raised the glass and tossed the contents into Don

Alfredo's face. He stepped behind the *haciendado*, grabbing him by his silver hair, pulling him to his feet as a shield, producing the Volcanic and putting it to his temple.

The three guards had spun towards him, aiming their carbines.

'Hold it!' Terrazos shouted. 'Unless you want me to spill his brains. You want me to? Put those guns down. Carefully now.'

'Do as he says,' Don Alfredo instructed. 'This mad dog has the upper hand for the moment.'

'I certainly have,' Terrazos grinned. 'Are you going to do as he says, or not?'

The guards reluctantly lowered their weapons and placed them on the stone floor. 'Kick them away.'

There was the sound of shooting and shouting echoing from the front of the house, women's screams, men's curses, children crying.

'What's going on?' Don Alfredo demanded.

'What do you think? You've had your

187

day.' Terrazos aimed his Volcanic at the guards, fired, sent one spinning, levered in a slug, took-out another, levered in another, cut the third guard down as he tried to run from the room. And returned the smoking barrel to the *haciendado*'s head as the explosions reverberated about the room. Rose, Jaime, and Don Alfredo watched with horror the last jerking spasms of the guards as their blood flowed.

'Stay where you are,' Terrazos spat at them as there was the sound of heavy boots along the passage. He raised the Volcanic in readiness, but it was two of his own *hombres* who charged in. 'It's OK, boys. No trouble here. Everything under control?'

'Yes, except for his damn screaming daughters and their spawn. We had to kill about six men. The rest are locked outside. How we gonna get out of here?'

'Easy. Kill that cripple first. We don't want nobody to tell the tale.'

'No!' Rose screamed, as one of the

carbines spat flame and death, and Jaime slumped forward, his head in a plate of food, blood trickling into the gravy. 'Stop this! Don't!'

Terrazos dragged the old man by his silver hair over to the wide, open window. He showed him through the bars to those outside. The *Comancheros* had taken up positions behind barrels, on the roof, in the loft of the stables, their rifles trained on him. 'You see!' Terrazos viciously shook the *haciendado* by his hair. 'This old fool has ruled over you for too long. I am taking over.'

He allowed this to sink in to the heads of the forty or so assembled *charros*, who had been joined by others running in from the ramparts, or racing in on horseback from the range when they heard the shooting.

'Yes, all of you, listen to what I have to say. I have killed Don Alfredo's son. I will do the same to him. With them dead, who will pay your wages? There will be no point in you attacking me. I am willing to share all we make from these cattle, the horses' — he brandished his arm out at the range, the corrals — 'among you. You can have anything you want in the house, in the cellars. Have his daughters, if you fancy them, the fat cows. I am taking the white girl to El Borracho. I will get a good price for her. Are you ready? Say goodbye to Don Alfredo.'

'No!' Rose screamed.

'*Si*. So long, old fool.' Terrazos blasted out a slug from the Volcanic and watched as blood and bone spattered, and Don Alfredo's brains, like grey bread sauce, spilled out into the courtyard below.

Even the hardened *Comancheros* gave a sigh of horror. But, again, Terrazos harangued them from the window. 'He is gone. Put up your guns. You do as I say from now on. Come on, *amigos*. We will open the door. Come in, split open one of his wine barrels, enjoy yourselves. The old rule is over.'

'*Basta!*' One of the men in the

courtyard sobbed, and raised his revolver to aim at Terrazos.

But, a man beside him turned his carbine on him, fired, and killed him. 'It makes sense,' he shouted, raising his weapon. 'Terrazos is our new chief, *hombres.*' There was a cheer of unison and the *Comancheros* surged towards the door of the *hacienda* intent on having a ball.

'My God!' Rose whispered. 'You are murderers, barbarians, all of you.'

'You theenk so?' Terrazos grinned at her, speaking his fractured English. He gripped her wrist and slapped her across the jaw. 'You happy to see me, again, eh?' He dragged her, screaming, towards the bedroom. 'You come weeth me.' He threw her into the room and turned to his comrades. '*Hombres*, your *generalissimo*, he no wan' to be disturbed for few minutes.' He gave a guttural laugh. 'Perhaps for a few hours, eh?'

11

The high adobe walls of Fort Sumner glowed pink and terracotta in the rays of the setting sun as Dawson rode towards the gates. He had covered the seventy miles from Los Portales in less than two days, and had left his young Ranger behind with Miguel and his small band of men to keep an eye on the Rancho del Oro. The gates of the blockhouse swung open as a sentry clanged a bell and he rode through into the dusty barracks square.

'I'm a Ranger out of Fort Worth, Texas,' he shouted to a trooper with three stripes on his sleeve. 'I need to talk to your commander.'

'Don't we all,' the sergeant drawled. 'You'll have a job gittin' through to him.'

Why became apparent when he was ushered into the office of Major Abraham Long. Short of stature and breath, unshaven, dishevelled, and sprawled over his desk, the major was killing his second bottle that day of Taos whiskey. Overweight and sweaty, he listened to Captain Dawson with cynical awe.

'A white gal, you say? Kidnapped and abused by the *Comancheros*? Tell me something new. Buddy, Uncle Sam's provided us with a couple of regiments to patrol the whole of this vast new territ'ry. We just got back from up north chasing Navajos. And now there's news of a band of Mescaleros causing mayhem down along the Pecos to the south. Fighting Indians is what we're paid to do. We've got to try to protect the damn fool emigrant trains heading West, and what few white settlers there are. Mister, I ain't got enough men to go round. An' I sure ain't got time to worry about one missing Texan gal.'

The major took a gulp of the whiskey and winced, shaking his head. 'Here, have a drink.' He pushed the bottle across and it wobbled on the edge of the table. 'If you can take it, that is?'

Ranger Dawson picked up the bottle, looked at it, and asked, 'So you're refusing to help me? All I'm asking for is a platoon of soldiers for a few days.'

'Out of the question.' Long shook his head back and forth, exaggeratedly. 'Aincha gonna have a bite outa that? If not, pass it back.'

Angrily, Dawson smashed the bottle against the desk. 'Pull yourself together, man. This poison will rot your brains. Isn't it your duty to protect civilians in distress?'

'You — ' Major Long stumbled to his feet, his palm outstretched. 'Thass my medicine. What you do that for? Where the hell'm I gonna get a drink from now? Thass my last bottle.'

'You won't get any courage from a bottle. Not that don't wear off in coupla hours. Nor no respect from your men.'

Long hammered the desk like a madman. 'Who the hell you think you are, some lousy Texan, comin' in here so high an' mighty, tellin' me what I oughta do, what I can drink?' Suddenly he buried his head in his arms and began sobbing. 'We lost four troopers Red Sleeves' last raid. You ever seen what a captive looks like after an Apache's had his fun? We could hardly recognize those boys.'

Dawson patted his shoulder, awkwardly. 'I seen what the Comanche does when they burn, rape and pillage. It ain't a pretty sight. But, it's no use dwelling on them things, Major. You just got to try an' do your best to protect others so it don't happen again.'

'Yeah, I guess.' Major Long fisted his reddened eyes, and tried to stand upright, fumbling at the buttons of his jacket. He buckled on his cavalry sabre and gun holster. 'We'll take what men I can spare, go take a look at the Rancho del Oro.' He looked up at the tall Ranger, an eager light in his eyes, and saluted. 'I guess you come all this way after one gal thass the least we can do.'

★　★　★

Joaquin Terrazos had spent a day roistering in the wine cellars of the late Don Alfredo, his men lurching noisily around, breaking open casks of liquor, drunkenly humiliating the old hidalgo's daughters. The second day, when they had sobered somewhat, he explained that the *vaqueros* would be divided up among his seven lieutenants, the *hombres* he had met in *Los Portales*, they would cut up the huge herd and drive it in various directions, to sell as beef to the emigrants passing through Las Vegas to the north *en route* to Santa Fe, to the army, or as stock to ranchers in the Pecos valley.

'You get what you can for the herds and you keep what you get,' he roared at them, loading his Volcanic. 'I will take this white woman' — he reached out and shook the pale and cowed Rose Cahill by her black curls — 'and two hundred of the broncos and sell them to *El Borracho*. Is that fair?'

'*Viva!*' — '*Vaya!*' — '*Ole!*' The *Comancheros* shouted as they went off under their sub-chiefs to cut out their herds. 'Terrazos, he is a good man!'

Numb and sore, terror lurking in her for what was yet to come, Rose was thrown onto a mustang and dragged along behind her captor as his *Comancheros*, bandannas up high against the stinging cloud of dust kicked up by more than the 200-head of half-wild broncos, drove them towards the west. Further and further away from her home she was taken, away from, she now believed, all possible hope of rescue.

For 100 miles and more they rode until they saw the shimmering plains of the Pecos valley, carpeted with grama grass as far as the eye could see, knee high on every hill and mesa, but frequented only by a few Mexican sheepherders and little communities of white emigrants willing to defy the Mescaleros' arrows.

They rested the horses amid the cottonwoods of the Bosque Redondo before riding on. In spite of her fear, her weariness, the cruel, jeering faces around her, Rose could not help but admire the awesome sweep of the wild country. Its *mélange* of earth reds, bright greens, and patches of Fall yellow against the great blue sky, its towering cumulus clouds hung over them. In any other company she would have rejoiced at the beauty of it all.

There was that other fear that was always with them, of Apache attack. The Mescalero and Jicarillo bands had ruled the country for centuries, descending from their mountain strongholds to rip the Spanish colonists apart by fire and lance. Little wonder that the Mexicans introduced *proyecto de guerra*, or scalp-hunting — $100 for a brave, £50 for a female, and $25 for a child. The evil of the bounty attracted the worst kind of renegades, white and Mexican, to the country. The Apaches countered with even more blood-curdling atrocities. The territory was virtually in a state of war.

However, the horse-drovers did not encounter any 'Messys', and rode on up a tributary of the Pecos, the Rio Hondo, towards a dark mountain wall dominated by the 3,000 ft hump of El Capitan. And Rose knew that somewhere among those ravines was the stronghold of the man known as *El Borracho*, reputed to be more cruel and vicious than even an Apache. The man she was destined to be wife or mistress to . . .

* * *

Miguel had hidden his small herd in a natural amphitheatre hollowed into the rocks — some said thousands of years before by the impact of a giant meteorite — near Los Portales. Pete had stayed with him and his small band of *charros* while Captain Dawson rode for help. Being young, he had quickly recovered from his ordeal in the desert, and had been provided with a spare boot and mustang.

When a detachment of US Cavalry arrived at the Rancho del Oro four days later they found the *hacienda* looted and deserted, apart from the females and grandchildren of the house, who were wailing and moaning, mourning Don Alfredo and his crippled son, the deaths of their husbands, and their own misfortune at the hands of the *Comancheros*.

'They've gawn,' Pete drawled, as he sat by the fountain in the courtyard, and watched the cavalry ride in. 'They split up the beeves and headed out.'

'Did you see Rose?' Captain Dawson sat his horse, removed his hat, and wiped his unruly hair away from his brow. 'Did she look . . . all right?' There was a catch in his voice as he asked the unnecessary question.

'Sure,' Miguel chimed in. 'She with Terrazos. He take two hundred broncos, head towards Bosque Grande.'

'Looks like you brought us on a wild goose chase.' The corpulent Major Long removed his campaign hat and wiped sweat from his forehead. 'And looks like a tornado hit this place.'

He went off to take a look at the cellars, and emerged with bottles of wine tucked under his arms. He eagerly uncorked one and began to glug it down. 'Gorgeous,' he gasped, wiping his mouth on the back of his hand. 'Thank the good Lord Don Alfredo kept a well-stocked cellar. There are a few bottles those lousy dagos overlooked.'

'Are you going after them, Major?' Dawson demanded.

'They've got a two-day start on us, man.'

'If they're driving two hundred horses we could catch up.'

Major Long was busy punishing the wine, knocking it back as if it was water, opening another bottle, shouting orders to his men to water their horses, cook up some rations, whatever they could find in the kitchens, if there was anything left that hadn't been stolen. 'You look like a damn dago, yourself,' he glowered at Dawson aggressively as the wine gave him Dutch courage. 'Why you wearing that sombrero, those leathers? I'm by no means certain you are a Ranger. That badge you showed me might have been stolen.'

It was true, his deep sunburn, his several weeks' growth of thick beard, his costume, gave him a malevolent air. If it weren't for his steady pale-grey eyes he might well have been taken for a Mexican. 'It was a disguise,' he said quietly. 'The only way we could get into the Cañon de Las Lagrimas.'

'Well, it ain't done you much good. If I were you I'd pack up an' go home. Wave goodbye to the little girlie. For Christ's sake, what good will she be to any man now?'

Dawson snatched hold of the major's coat uniform and raised his clenched fist, his face set. But he relaxed, let him go. 'I ain't givin' up. Are you gonna help us, or not?'

'I've done all I can. I've got more important things to worry about than one stolen gal.' He turned away, took another swig of the vintage. 'Us Yanks bit off more than we could chew out here. The government's trying to run things on the cheap. I'm completely over-stretched.'

'You wanna buy cows, meester?' Miguel piped up.

'Cows?' The little major spun on him. 'Stolen, no doubt?'

'No, *señor*. Only from the Texans.'

'In that case, why not? We're in need of fresh meat at the fort.' The major leered at Dawson. 'Damn Texans. They'll be our enemies soon enough. There's a war hotting up.'

Dawson turned away, dunked his head under the fountain, washed away some of the dust, the disappointment, left Miguel and the major to their bargaining. He flicked his hair from his eyes and patted Pete on the shoulder. 'How about you, *amigo*?'

'Sure, I'm ready to ride, Cap.'

'We'll leave at dawn.'

★ ★ ★

From the Pecos they rode 150 miles up the Hondo and the Rio Bonito, into the rugged hills until they saw El Capitan towering over them. At night Rose was bedded down with the other girls, Juana and Celeste, and Louisa, an innocent-looking granddaughter of Don Alfredo of about fifteen. Terrazos was proud of the fact that the latter was a virgin and he did not plan to throw her or Rose to his *vaquero* dogs. In peach condition they would bring a fine price. Nonetheless, at night they were roped together like hobbled horses, and they huddled into each other both for comfort and warmth against the cold wind.

Terrazos had sold a good many of the broncos to small ranches as they went along, but he still had a bunch of fifty to herd before them. As they were climbing them up a steep ravine a rifle shot cracked, and a bullet whined close to their heads, the explosion clapping off the cliff walls. They looked up and saw the glint of the sun on rifle barrel, and another rifleman showed himself on a ledge. '*Ola! Que quiere usted?*' he shouted. '*Quien es usted?*'

'*Amigo. No tiras.* We have girls for El Borracho.'

The guard beckoned them forward, and they climbed on up the narrow ravine, more and more *bandidos* showing themselves on the cliffs of a more or less impregnable mesa where a high-walled adobe fortress had been built into the side of the cliff. From thorn bushes nearby the heads of Apaches dangled, sickeningly. The horses rattled up onto a stretch of stony tableland, to be corralled by the *vaqueros*. A giant of a man, with a bushy, grey-streaked beard, stepped from an entranceway. He was carrying a carbine, with a revolver hung on his hip. He swaggered up to the girls straddling their horses, windswept, their legs bare, their dresses hitched up. He gripped Rose's calf in his grimy hand, and jerked her from the mustang's back. She hit the ground hard, gasping at the impact, her knees and elbows grazed.

El Borracho gave a great roar of laughter and hauled her to her feet by her hair. He squeezed her face between thumb and forefinger and his black eyes burned into her. 'Well,' he growled. 'What have we here?'

'The finest Texas rose,' Joaquin Terrazos grinned, his gold teeth glinting greedily. 'I have brought her all the way from Fort Worth just for you. Isn't she just what you wanted?' He pulled apart her dress. 'Look at that milk-white skin.'

'A beauty,' El Borracho grunted, and Rose flinched as he fondled her. 'You have done well.'

'In prime condition, untouched. I ask only a thousand dollars as it is you.'

'A beauty for a beast.' The barrel-chested man roared with laughter again, and glanced along the line of girls. 'And who are these?'

'These two were Don Alfredo's personal *putas*. The very best. Five hundred each. And this one' — he reached the lustrous-eyed, terrified Mexican girl and stroked her thigh — 'she is a virgin, I promise you. None other than Don Alfredo's granddaughter, the blood of a marquis of Spain running in her veins. Surely worth another thousand, eh?'

'Don Alfredo's granddaughter?' El Borracho scratched at a sweat-stained woollen vest, black with dirt and torn, that clung to his vast belly. His legs were encased in baggy cotton tucked into heavy, spurred boots. 'But how is this? Don Alfredo would not sell his granddaughter.'

'He didn't. I killed him. Blew his brains out. I am the *gran commandante* of all the *Comancheros* now' — he gave a twitchy smile — 'after you, that is.'

'You killed him?' El Borracho's voice boomed out. 'But Don Alfredo was a friend of mine.'

Joaquin Terrazos fingered his vivid scar, shrugged uncomfortably, backing away a pace, looking around at the gathered *bandidos*. 'You know how it is.

These things happen. Don Alfredo was old. He got on my nerves. We needed a new man. All the others have agreed . . . I am their chief.'

El Borracho glowered at him, raising and cocking his carbine one-handed, pointing it at Joaquin Terrazos's chest. Then he gave another roar of laughter, slapping his shoulder, nearly knocking him over. 'That scared you, eh? You nearly shit yourself.' He slapped him again. 'You did right. What do I care about that old goat? *Amigo*, bring the women inside.'

12

To the west, through a breach in the iron-black mountains, the setting sun glowed and flickered like a blacksmith's forge. As darkness came on they made camp amid a clump of tangy junipers, Pete and Captain Dawson alone, for Miguel had herded his cattle to the fort to pick up $2,000 in gold coin for the 400 at $5 a head — 'none of this yere paper money', as the folk in these parts said. In this remote area the two Rangers had encountered few travellers on the trail, only dark and weathered Mexicans in cotton rags and rope-soled slippers driving caravans of burros a'totter with stacks of goathides or rope for sale. They carried water in the skins of hogs with cowhorn spigots, and, with their ragged women and children, whipped their poor animals hurriedly past the two horsemen. Perhaps they thought they were *Comancheros*.

They were leaned back against their saddles, their bellies full, digesting part of a roasted antelope, the captain silent and brooding as he stared into the flames, when they heard the clip of horsemen approaching, quickly reached for their revolvers and kneeled in readiness.

'Hello the camp,' a man called, reining in his mount. 'Can we come in?'

'Who goes there?'

'Christopher Carson, Indian agent, on government business.'

'Come forward,' Dawson shouted. 'Step down.'

'That smells mighty appetizing.' The rider was wearing the fringed buckskins of a frontiersman, with a slouch hat. A sturdy fellow, of average height, five eight or so, and in his fifties. 'Any to spare?'

'Help yourself,' Dawson said, keeping them covered with his six-gun while he inspected Carson and his six companions by the glow of the fire. 'Where you from?'

'I superintend the Ute reservations back across the mountains,' Carson said, carving himself a haunch of venison, and sitting cross-legged to eat with his hands. 'We had our sheep raided by Mangas Colorado. We're on his trail.'

'Red Sleeves? The Mimbreno?'

'Yes, a bloodthirsty butcher, indeed. He's got to be punished, or there'll never be any peace in this land.'

His men were too busy hogging the remains of the venison to say much, and Carson, as he ate, listened to the Ranger's story. 'El Borracho, you say? Ha! Fat chance you have against that murderer. He sits up in his eagle's nest only venturing out to plunder the countryside and cause mayhem. He's half the cause of our troubles with yon Apache.'

'How so?' Dawson filled his own cup with coffee and passed it across, and Pete did likewise for one of the others.

Carson took his time answering, tossing a bone away, and supping the scalding brew through his moustache. 'He was with that bastard Englishman, Johnson, when they invited four hundred of Red Sleeve's people to a feast down at Santa Rita, then opened up on 'em with a howitzer. Scalphunters. A lot of innocent settlers have died as a result of the treachery of them two. Mangas Colorado has been on the warpath ever since. He's an old man now, must be over sixty, but he's still a formidable warrior. You can't miss him if you see him. He's six foot six, unusual for a 'Pache'.

'Bigger they are, harder they fall,' one of the men growled.

'Yea, many of the mighty have fallen,' Carson agreed. 'The Mimbrenos are fierce fighters but they can be tamed. There's only one way to do that, by starvation, fire and sword. Bring the army in. Show 'em we're the new masters of this land.'

Dawson stroked his beard thoughtfully. 'Ain't I heard of you? Kit Carson, the scout, the man who drove three thousand head of sheep from these parts to California to sell to the gold-miners ten years back?'

'That's me. Made a pretty packet, too,'

There was another racket of hooves riding up the trail, the dark shapes of men, and they all grabbed instinctively for their guns. 'Who's this?' Carson asked.

'It's Miguel. Friend of mine,' Dawson said. 'He's been to sell his cows to the fort. He's OK.'

'Aiyee!' Miguel shouted, the light shining on his bald head as he crouched beside them. 'We ride hard to catch you. We no want to mees the fight.'

'You'll have a durn hard job flushing El Borracho out of his eyrie. Nobody's succeeded yet. How many are you? Eight? He's got at least thirty or forty of those damn *Comancheros* hiding out with him up there.'

'We can try,' Dawson gritted out,

gloomily, but he, too, had his doubts.

'Well, gentlemen, I wish you luck. I understand El Borracho is selling Apache heads these days, rather than scalps. More profitable, it seems. He dries and shrinks them. Those who buy ain't choosy which tribe they come from, peaceful or hostile. They just want a souvenir.'

'Yeah,' one of his men spat out, 'an he's turned whoremonger, too, selling concubines across the border.'

'They're not all whores,' Dawson said, but nobody was listening.

Carson and his men were getting up to remount. 'We're going on after Mangas Colorado.'

'*Señor*, you want a snort before you go?' Miguel yelled, raising a flagon of Don Alfredo's rum.

'Never touch the stuff,' Carson retorted.

They watched as he led his men away into the night.

★　★　★

Mangas Colorado and his war party were not waiting for the renowned Indian punisher, Kit Carson, and his men to catch up. They had turned their ponies and doubled back to give him the slip, and early the next dawn were heading up the white-man's trail beneath the shadow of El Capitan. Imagine their delight when they saw a party of what they took to be Mexicans breakfasting among some junipers! They had a bone to pick with *Comancheros*. And there were only eight of them to their band of thirty-five braves.

The first Chas Dawson knew of them was when he heard a strangulated gasp and looked up to see one of Miguel's *vaqueros* clutching at a greasewood arrow that had gone clean through his throat, in one side, out the other. And then arrows were hissing past his head, as he grabbed at his Sharps and rolled for cover. A mustang shrieked as a lance penetrated its side, and it rolled, hooves kicking the air.

Simultaneously, there was a blood-curdling war-cry and a grey-haired Apache came galloping towards them. He wheeled his stallion, its hooves pawing the air, stood tall in the saddle and hurled his iron-tipped spear. It penetrated the back of another of Miguel's men who was running for the bushes. He fell clawing the earth.

Dawson's Sharps barked out as he took aim at the Mimbreno war chief in his red shirt and cotton trousers tucked into knee-length moccasins. But, it was obviously not Red Sleeves's day to die for the bullet missed him by some miracle, and Dawson, himself, had to duck as an arrow creased his scalp.

The warrior galloped back to join his braves, some of whom were running forward on foot firing their arrows faster than Miguel's men could reload their single shots. But, by now, they had jumped into the cover of a nest of rocks and were giving as good as they got. Two Mimbrenos stumbled and gave up the ghost as their bullets crashed out.

After a while an uncanny silence reigned. Red Sleeves was not having it as easy as he had hoped. Whenever he or his warriors tried to run in close they were met by a hail of lead. He would play the waiting game. Soon the *pinda-lickoyees* — the white eyes — would have to run out of ammunition and he and his braves would be able to get to close quarters to finish them.

Miguel took the opportunity of the lull to reach for the two sacks of gold coins he had left beside the fire. He crawled back and hid them in holes in the rocks. '*Amigos*, they no getting their hands on thees,' he grinned, rubbing his bald pate. 'Even if they do take my hair.'

'Maybe we could parley,' Pete suggested, as he lay beside the Captain, Miguel and his three remaining men. He peered through the rocks and began to reload his Smith & Wesson. He only had one carton of a dozen bullets left. 'We cain't hold out here for ever, thass for sure.'

'Parley with Mimbrenos? Pah! You joking, *amigo*? They don' parley with no one.'

'Anyone speak any 'Pache?' Dawson muttered.

'*Si*, a leetle,' Miguel said, 'but it no damn use. What we must do is make every shot tell.'

'Shout out we want to talk. Tell him we're friends. Tell him we hate the scalphunters of Apaches. Say we have come many miles, two moons' journey from far away, to attack El Borracho and Joaquin Terrazos, and to rescue the white squaws they have stolen from us.'

'Sure, you theenk he take any notice of that? He would as soon cut thees ladies up as us.'

'Try. Tell him if he helps us we will pay him in gold.'

'Gold?' Miguel tugged at his long moustache ends, angrily. 'What gold?'

'Yours. You want to stay alive, don't you?'

'*Si*, I guess,' Miguel sighed. 'I can try.' And he began to holler out words in the hissing glottal mumbo-jumbo of Apache with all its 'zl' and 'tz' twists, mixed with Spanish and odd *Americano* which the Apaches might understand.

'*Neutsche-schee*,' he warbled, as if he might have something stuck in his throat. 'Come over here, *amigo*.'

There was another eerie silence while the Mimbrenos chewed this over. Mangas Colorado had already lost four braves and it was likely he might lose more if he tried to bring this fight to a brief conclusion. And what the white eyes had to say interested him. Before he turned renegade he had helped the *Americanos* in their war with the Mexicans. Some of them could be trusted, if very few. He would give it a chance for the gods had smiled on them so far on this raid and it seemed to be a good day.

'He's coming forward. Hold your fire.' Dawson watched the big Mimbreno warrior, unbowed by age, amble his stallion forward at a walk, his arm raised in peace. His dark eroded face was hard set, his eyes smouldering fiercely, his long grey hair tied back by a crimson headband. Dawson rose from the rocks and raised his own hand. 'Welcome,' he said.

Mangas Colorado stopped his stallion with his knees twenty paces away and hissed some reply, his eyes inquisitive now. 'Tell him I am a Texan, from a land beyond that of the Comanches. I have no quarrel with him.'

Miguel stood beside him in his purple serape, his carbine in his hand, and began spitting out words like a hissing snake. 'I say I have magic. I make gold come out of rocks. I tell him he can buy many guns, much whiskey with this yellow metal.'

'I ain't in the business of running guns to the Indians,' Dawson protested. 'But, well, I guess he can use it as he wishes. We cain't stop him, can we?'

The old Mimbreno's eyes had taken on a spark of curiosity. And he had signalled his braves to come creeping forward. They did so, arrows taut in their bows, a harsh-looking bunch, most in baggy shirts and breech-clouts, with long tail cloths fore and aft, their muscular thighs blackened by the sun.

'Show us this magic,' Red Sleeves shouted in Apache.

'If we do, you help us attack El Borracho?' Dawson pointed his Sharps up at El Capitan, and waited as Miguel translated the words.

Mangas Colorado nodded, thudded a fist to his chest and shouted out hissing words, and Miguel grinned, waved his carbine about in the air and plucked a sack of gold coins from the rocks. The Mimbrenos gave a gasp of surprise as he tossed it to their leader. The old chieftain shook it and peered inside. He gave a yell of triumph and raised it over his head.

'I no geev him the other one,' Miguel said. 'I need that if I ever get out of this mess. He ees satisfied. He say we will fight.'

It was still early dawn. Miguel offered

the Mimbrenos the *jarre* of rum to put them in a fighting mood, and the revolvers and rifles of his fallen men, and let them fight over the share-out. They left the corpses where they lay, and saddled their horses. '*Andale, amigos,*' Miguel shouted, and spurred his mustang away.

The Mimbrenos leapt onto their mustangs and sped after the little band of Texans and Mexicans. For many long years they had hated the scalphunter and killer El Borracho and here were ones ready to lead them against him.

'This ain't gonna be easy,' Dawson said, as he halted his horse and stared up a narrow ravine. Mangas Colorado pointed a finger and screamed out words of hatred. Halfway up the mountain they could see some kind of adobe structure like a Navajo pueblo built into the cliff. 'We're gonna have to fight every foot of the way up that arroyo.'

'Ain't there another way up?' Pete asked as, in his snakeskin jacket and flared trousers, he sat his spirited mustang and pointed to the rear of the cliff.

Mangas Colorado looked at his men, and one of them nodded. As one they turned and galloped off the trail, heading through the scrub. Dawson and his men chased after them.

'Maybe we should wait 'til night?' Pete said, as they dismounted and tethered their horses. They were about two miles around the base of the mountain.

'The 'Pache are the same as the Comanch'. They won't fight at night,' Dawson said. 'Scared of the ghosts. It's now or never.'

The Mimbreno who had led the way was running up the mountainside with one of the dead Mexican's rifles in his hands. The other of the thirty-strong band went darting on foot after him, bounding across the rocks like antelopes.

'Come on,' Dawson cried. 'It's gonna be a helluva job keeping up with these boys.'

They were already out of breath

when they caught up with the Apaches who had paused beneath a sheer precipice. One of them beside Mangas Colorado was pointing upwards. The chief turned to Dawson and for the first time a smile spread over his face as he slung his new carbine over his back and shouted, '*Venga!*'

'We ain' goin' up there, are we?' Miguel crossed himself as he watched the Apaches climb up along a fault in the cliff, hanging by their fingers and toes as they edged their way higher. They reached a shelf of rock and went bounding on, climbing like goats.

'It would be easier if we took our boots off,' Pete said, and sat down to do so. 'At least, I'm going to.' The others followed suit, cutting bits of a lariat to tie their boots together and slinging them around their necks. 'Wish me luck.' Pete began to pick his way up the fault. High above him the Mimbrenos were already disappearing from sight. Only a couple of dislodged rocks that nearly knocked him from his perch showed the way they had gone. 'Those boys sure know how to climb.'

It was a long, precarious struggle. The only thing to do was keep on climbing, hanging like a fly to a wall across the sheer cliff, trying not to look down, reach a resting point and searching for another path up. Higher and higher Pete climbed, glancing back to see Dawson not far behind, his face intent as he manoeuvred around a buttress. There was a sudden scream from below. One of the Mexicans had slipped. He went sailing through the air, his *serape* outspread, a bird who could not fly, to land 1,000 feet below, tumbling and bouncing down the shale to lie still.

The young Texan gave a whistle of awe as he reached out a hand to help Dawson join him. 'Only hope that yell didn't alert them on top.' He looked up and saw the dark thighs of the Apaches as they scrambled over a ledge. 'It ain't far now, Cap.'

'Good.' For moments Dawson retained

the youth's grasp. 'If anything happens, well, kid, you've proved a damn fine Ranger. I'm proud of you.'

Pete blinked at him, for some reason, through sudden tears. 'I'm proud of you, Cap.'

'Come on,' Dawson said, helping Miguel to join them. 'We can do this.'

The Mimbrenos were flattened to the ground waiting for them as they reached the cliff-top. Mangas Colorado pointed his rifle forward silently and Dawson saw that they had judged the climb well. The cliff ledge, which was a dead end at this point, opened out to a wide promontory on which were corralled bunches of horses. A group of *Comancheros* were sitting around a fire making a leisurely breakfast by the look of it. Others seemed to come from the face of the cliff to join them. That was where the adobe dwelling would be.

'Every man for himself,' he shouted. 'Fire at will.' He fed a slug into the breech of his Sharps and took out one of the men around the fire. He sent another spinning to topple over the cliff before the *bandidos* realized what was happening. With shrill cries, the Mimbrenos went leaping and dodging into the attack as lead began to whistle their way. The surprised *Comancheros* were pulling out revolvers, blamming wildly at them, and falling under a hail of arrows.

Captain Chas Dawson went haring after the Mimbrenos, firing his carbine from the hip and, when he had no time to reload, cracking it across the head of a Mexican who ran to tackle him. He drew his revolver, and stood to assess the scene as more *Comancheros* ran from the stables and the adobe building and some of the Apache took their last fall, caught in a vitriolic cross-fire.

Mangas Colorado, his one shot spent, was swinging his rifle like a battle axe, tumbling attackers like ninepins. Dawson saw a *Comanchero* take careful aim to put a bullet in the warrior's back and he cut him down with a revolver shot before he could do so. A withering rifle fire was pouring from the portholes of the 'dobe high above the doorway and others of the Apache screamed as it caught them.

'How the hell we gonna flush 'em out of there without hurting the wimmin?' the captain muttered.

Pete, beside him, said, 'There's only one way; we gotta go in.' And he dashed for the doorway. His revolver spurted death as he met a *Comanchero*, and he jumped over his body.

Dawson followed, leaving Miguel and his remaining men to trade lead with the *Comancheros* while, with ear-splitting howls the Mimbrenos engaged in hand-to-hand combat, knives flashing, skullcrackers thudding bloodily, lances thrusting, as they leaped into the affray in the morning sunshine.

Dawson crouched low and ran after the young Texan, diving into the doorway as bullets splintered the wall about him, for guards were running up from the ravine. In the cave-like darkness of the house he stepped aside as a Mexican came scrambling down a steep staircase. He stuck out a foot to trip him and bludgeoned him with the revolver butt. Up above, Pete was doing the same thing, fighting his way up the stairs.

Dawson clambered over the bodies and reached a landing. The place was like a maze, with smaller rooms and stairways leading off a central area which appeared to be filled with gunpowder barrels, guns and ammunition. It was a good job they had had the element of surprise. The *bandidos* could have held out for months locked in here. A blazing tar torch illumined the interior gloom, and he snatched it, thrust it in the face of a man who stepped out at him, a machete raised. The man screamed as his beard caught alight. Dawson twisted the machete from his grasp and cut him down with it. He swung it to chop across the throat of another thug who moved out of the shadows to get him. Blood gouted as the attacker went down on his knees.

Persistent shooting was coming from the floor above. Pete had disappeared down one of the corridors and Dawson saw flashes of gunfire from that direction. He picked up a wooden ladder and propped it against the third ledge of the landing. He was nearly to the top, climbing unsteadily, machete in one hand, revolver in the other, when he saw a man standing above him, a man with a vivid white scar on his cheek, his teeth flashing in an evil leer. Dawson was caught cold, at his mercy. He tried to raise his revolver, but Terrazos kicked the ladder away. For seconds Dawson hung sickeningly in space as Terrazos aimed the big Volcanic at him. The explosion boomed out as Dawson slipped and fell, the bullet missing him by inches. He hit the ground hard, and lay, the wind knocked out of his body. Terrazos laughed, levered in another ball, and aimed again. This time he couldn't miss.

But another shot rang out. And Joaquin Terrazos stood poised for seconds on his toes, his grin turning into a grimace of pain and anger. He clutched at his chest. Then he tumbled in a somersault down, crashing on his back beside the captain. Dawson severed his head with one swipe of the machete — to make sure. He looked up and saw Pete standing, his nickel-plated S & W smoking.

The boy glanced at him, anxiously. 'You OK, Cap?'

'Yeah. Thanks to you. The other one's still up there. Watch it. He's dangerous.'

Pete returned his spent Smith & Wesson to his holster, picked up the Volcanic, and replaced the ladder. As another bandit appeared on the landing he fired and he, too, toppled down. But he was only a nondescript, skinny *Comanchero*. The other one was up there in his lair. And he had the women with him for they suddenly heard a shrill scream.

The youth crept up the ladder. How

the hell, he wondered, was he to get at El Borracho without hurting the women? He reached the top and scrambled over the ledge, then crept, at a squat, towards the flickering shadows of another room. He could hear the rustle of dresses, even the sound of breathing, a man's guttural voice telling them to stay silent. He guessed the lousy coward would be using them as a shield. And it proved true when he lunged forwards through the doorway, firing high over the heads as he did so.

The gargantuan El Borracho was not expecting someone to come flying in at floor level. He had one thick arm around Rose Cahill's throat, his filthy beard in her face, her body pressed to his great sweating carcasse, and a .45 in his paw. The other three Spanish girls were lined up in front of him under pain of death, but now they shrieked and leapt aside like startled chickens as El Borracho emptied the revolver at the youth.

Rose gripped his massive arm and

struggled with him, and as the Texan youth rolled across the floor, managed to make the Mexican leader miss with every shot. She bit into his arm as he cursed and threw her aside. He fell on the boy, pinning him to the ground, twice his weight, twisting the Volcanic from his grip.

Pete struggled, but knew he had no chance as the great hairy hands gripped his throat, choking out his life, and all he could emit was a croaking sound as he looked up into beady, red-rimmed eyes, the puffy face in its greasy, grey beard, the thick lips beginning to spread into a gloating grin. And then he glimpsed the flash of a machete, and blood spouting from the thick neck and, as El Borracho's grip weakened, the captain standing there, and hacking the machete from the other side so that the great head suddenly toppled to one side and the mouth opened in a scream. Dawson, maddened, hacked and hacked again, until the head rolled free. Then he stood there gasping and shuddering as Rose Cahill ran into his arms, clinging to him, and sobbing, 'He's dead now. He's dead.'

Blood-soaked, Pete got to his feet groggily, feeling at his throat. 'Whoo,' he croaked out. 'That was a close one. Thanks, Cap.'

Charles Dawson stood there, the machete dangling from his grasp, pulling Rose Cahill into him, tight, as if he could never let her go. He looked like a man who'd been to hell and back.

Pete looked out of the small window. 'I think it's all over,' he said. The last of the bandits were scrambling onto mustangs, and clattering away down the ravine as fast as they could, bullets whistling about their ears. And the Mimbreno warriors were running about, their scalping knives flashing, finishing off the wounded, taking bloody trophies, waving them to the skies in triumph. 'We've won the day, Cap.'

He grinned at the pretty Mexican

girls who were chattering and comforting each other. 'OK, *muchachas*, you're safe now. You're free.' And he went bounding down out of the wall house to see what was going on.

When Captain Dawson came down to stand in the doorway he still had his arm around Rose Cahill. They watched the Mimbrenos looting the bodies for guns, rounding up the mustangs and, leaping onto their own ponies, herd them with shrill cries down the ravine.

Mangas Colorado rode a captured mustang up to them, his dark face stern, brandishing his carbine over his head, shouting out words. Dawson saluted, and the old chieftain went jogging away after his men.

'He said 'thank you, Texan',' Miguel said, limping towards them, his bald head shining in the sun. 'He said if you go through his land you have his protection. He wishes you and your squaw well.'

'A good thing he didn't come inside or he would have found all these guns and powder. I guess he's in a hurry to get back to his village before Carson picks up his trail,' Dawson said, watching Red Sleeves go. 'He's a fine warrior. We wouldn't have done this without him. It's funny, in many ways I wish him well, too.'

13

'Watcha gonna do now?' Pete asked, as they rode back around the mountain to collect their hitched horses. 'I mean, I guess we gotta take you back to Don Alfredo's place. You got kin there?'

'Pah! My mangy aunts. Always purring and squabbling like fat cats.' The bright-eyed Mexican girl was very forthright in her opinions as she jogged along beside him. 'All their men been killed. I dunno what they gonna do. They won't want me. Another mouth to feed.'

'They won't?' A spark ignited unthought of hope in the young Texan. He was very taken by the pretty young *señorita*. In fact, the first flash of her eyes had set his heart pounding worse than if he were going into a gunfight. 'Maybe — if the cap agrees — you could come back with us to Texas?'

'Texas?' she laughed. 'Why should I go to Texas?'

'There's a Mex rancher I worked for awhile, horse rancher, near San Antone. He lost his only daughter with the cholera. He's a nice ole fella. He might like to give you a home, you know, adopt you.'

'Really? That sounds good. But why — '

'I could have a word with him. An', when I get leave from being a Ranger, I could call an' see you.'

'Ai-yai-yi!' she smiled. 'Could it be that it is you who wants me to come to Texas?'

'Could be,' he mumbled, reddening beneath his tan, as he slipped from the saddle to pick up the reins of the waiting horses. He looked at the sheer 1,000 ft cliff and whistled. 'Look at that. Can you believe we climbed up there to rescue four darn females?'

Louisa slid from her horse to stand beside him in the shadow of the cliff. 'Do you believe in destiny, Pete?' she whispered.

'Destiny? You mean it was sorta meant for me to climb up there, to meet you?' They were jammed close between two broncs. In fact, he had never been so close to a gal before. He swallowed his fear, reached out hands for her slender waist, pulled her to him and kissed her. It was a strange experience, kissing. He wanted to go on and on. And the funny thing was she did not seem averse to putting her lips and body close to his.

'Maybe it was,' she murmured as they broke for a breather. 'Destiny.'

Suddenly an elation hit him. It didn't seem possible. Could this be that thing they were always talking and singing about but nobody knew what it meant? 'Yee-hoo!' he yelled, picking her up and placing her back on her pony. 'Less git back an' ask Cap if it's OK you come with us.'

'Señor Pete,' she laughed. 'What has got into you?'

'I dunno,' he grinned. 'All I know is I cain't wait 'til *mañana*.'

They rode back at a gallop driving the spare broncs and as they climbed the ravine heard a colossal explosion, a fountain of rocks showering out from where the old pueblo had been. 'Jeez!' he shouted. 'He musta dropped a match or sumpun.'

By the time they reached the top, the pueblo was just a pile of rubble amid the settling dust and Miguel and the captain were shouting, excitedly. When Pete reached them, Miguel was on his knees running his hands through a casket of gold coins. '*Caramba*! We are reech. I will buy myself a *rancho*! A saloon! A new sombrero!'

'This must be where El Borracho kept his ill-gotten gains,' Captain Dawson said. 'When we blew the place up there it was hid in the wall.'

'Why you blow it up?' Louisa asked.

'Ach, girlie. There's too many guns, rifles and ammo in this territory. A few less will be doing somebody a favour. So I put a fuse to them barrels of gunpowder.'

'Cap, is it OK if Louisa comes back with us?'

'Sure. Why not? If she wants to.' He smiled at the girl and said, 'You know, this character may only be fourteen, but in my book he's proved himself to be a man. You couldn't do better hanging on to him.'

'Don' you worry, Captain.' Her eyes danced as she met Pete's. 'I already peek heem out for branding.'

★ ★ ★

They shouted 'adios' to Miguel and his men, who with gold in their saddle-bags, the other hidden sack to retrieve, and the heads of El Borracho and Joaquin Terrazos in fly-buzzing gunny sacks, were in fine fettle as they headed back to Fort Sumner to claim the rewards on the badmen.

Captain Dawson, Rose, Louisa, and Pete Bowen headed their mustangs and pack horses south-west towards the peaks of the Sierra Blanca. They had a

241

long journey before them, climbing the pass through the Sacramento Mountains and down the Tularosa River. Occasionally they sighted bands of Apache horsemen on the hilltops, and glanced, anxiously, at each other. It seemed smoke messages had been sent. The Indians merely watched them as they passed. They bided a night in the Hispanic village of Tularosa at the foot of the mountains, and there, amid much fiesta, Captain Dawson and Rose were wed in the mission church.

That night they lay together, listening to the strains of guitars, the dancing, the singing, and Rose turned to him, her face anguished beneath her mass of black curls. 'I shouldn't have married you, Chas,' she sobbed. 'I'm not worthy of you. Those men — '

'You've got to try to forget them, Rose,' the Ranger said. 'I know what you been through. You married a man who treated you bad. You been defiled by, what, three men you despised and hated. Ain't that right?' His shirt was damp with her tears as she nodded her agreement. 'So,' he said, gripping her to him. 'This time you gonna be loved. If a man loves a woman it don't matter to him what been done to her in the past. It's gonna be all right.'

'Oh, Chas.' She smiled up at him through her tears. 'It will be. I know it will.'

★ ★ ★

But they didn't have much time to be lovey-dovey. Across the river was a flat barren desert strewn with black lava. Along the edge of the glittering White Sands, and up through the San Augustin Pass dividing the Organ and San Andreas mountains they made their tortuous way. A hard ride they had of it before they reached the Rio Grande and arrived in El Paso. They were back in Texas.

It so happened the trans-continental Butterfield stage was due to arrive, so they sold their broncs, much to the

243

girls' relief, had hot baths, and a meal of buffalo hump and red hot chillis that nearly blew their brains out, and rode in style in the comfort of the hammock-slung Concorde coach all the way across Texas to Fort Worth.

'We can live at Jake's farm,' Rose said. 'I mean, I guess it's mine now.'

'Hell, no. I got enough stolen gold to buy myself my own spread along the Brazos,' Dawson grinned. 'Ranger, I'm giving you four weeks' furlough to escort that gal down to San Antone. Then I expect to see you back here at the fort and ready for duty. We got Comanches to fight.'

'Yessuh, Cap.' Pete saluted, snapping his boot heels. 'Sure thang.'

As they left Colonel Jesse Frampton's office he gave a whoop, whirled Louisa and yelled, 'Four weeks! We gonna have us a party.'

Afterword

Their happiness, as many others, was short-lived. The black clouds of war rolled over Texas. Captain Chas Dawson chose to stay in the Rangers to protect the homesteads, women and children left exposed to marauding Comanches as their men enrolled to fight for the South. In '64 he resigned his commission honourably, settled down with Rose to ranching, and was one of the first to roll his herds north.

The clarion call of war was answered, too, by young Pete Bowen. He joined Wharton's Texan brigade, fought through the hell of Shiloh, and was in Kentucky with Forrest's Raiders. At the age of 17 he was commissioned first lieutenant and led the Cherokee rebel cavalry in Indian Territory in a bitter, losing campaign. With war's end he refused to surrender and rode across the American desert to Nevada to seek his fortune in the gold mines of Virginia City (see *Lousy Reb*). A year later he returned to Texas via the Territory (*Bushwhacked*) to marry Louisa and they settled a ranch on the border, raising a son and fighting Comanche (*Death at Sombrero Rock*).

Life was not easy for the Westerner now known as Black Pete Bowen. When Louisa was murdered he killed the cattle baron responsible, sent his son to an aunt in the East and turned outlaw. He rode both sides of the law in Colorado (*Duel at Silverillo*) and in Kansas (*Quantrill Raiders*). He was both US Marshal and bank robber. He fought for revolutionaries in Mexico (*Bullwhip*) where his second wife was stolen from him (*Bad Day at San Juan*). He was not lucky in love, for a third Spanish girl he fell for died in his arms as he helped defend her father's *hacienda* (*The Crooked Sheriff*). But there was always another woman, another town, more trouble as he drifted across the high plains, (*The Train Robbers, Rogue Railroad*) in the lawless 1870s.

By now a legendary gunfighter, he was beginning to get old and have trouble with his eyes when he married an Indian girl. He led a gang of rustlers (*Black Pete — Outlaw*) before settling down to homestead in Montana. And raised a half-caste brood, becoming a respected rancher, before taking up his guns, alongside his daughter, to fight for justice once again (*The Horse Dreamer*).

The author thinks that, now his story has been told, from boyhood to middle age, it is time to put Black Pete out to pastures of clover. And may the old war-horse enjoy his retirement!

As for Mangas Colorado, history records that he was captured by the army in '63, tortured with red-hot bayonets, and 'shot attempting to escape'.

We do hope that you have enjoyed reading this large print book.

Did you know that all of our titles are available for purchase?

We publish a wide range of high quality large print books including:
**Romances, Mysteries, Classics
General Fiction
Non Fiction and Westerns**

Special interest titles available in large print are:
**The Little Oxford Dictionary
Music Book, Song Book
Hymn Book, Service Book**

Also available from us courtesy of Oxford University Press:
**Young Readers' Dictionary
(large print edition)
Young Readers' Thesaurus
(large print edition)**

For further information or a free brochure, please contact us at:
**Ulverscroft Large Print Books Ltd.,
The Green, Bradgate Road, Anstey,
Leicester, LE7 7FU, England.
Tel:** (00 44) **0116 236 4325**
Fax: (00 44) **0116 234 0205**

CABEL

Paul K. McAfee

Josh Cabel returned home from the Civil War to find his family all murdered by rioting members of Quantrill's band. The hunt for the killers led Josh to Colorado City where, after months of searching, he finally settled down to work on a ranch nearby. He saved the life of an Indian, who led him to a cache of weapons waiting for Sitting Bull's attack on the Whites. His involvement threw Cabel into grave danger. When the final confrontation came, who had the fastest — and deadlier — draw?

BLACK RIVER

Adam Wright

John Dyer has come to the insignificant little town of Black River to destroy the last living reminder of his dark past. He has come to kill. Jack Hart is determined to stop him. Only he knows the terrible truth that has driven Dyer here, and he knows that only he can beat Dyer in a gunfight. Ex-lawman Brad Harris is after Dyer too — to avenge his family. The stage is set for madness, death and vengeance.